To Be Honest

&

Of Good

Report

W. R. Hanson

To the memory of my mother, who was my first reader.

Names & Places.

Chan Hong-Chun, aka Jeremy, was not Eur-Asian. Both of his parents were Chinese-Malay. "Jeremy" had been no pin-in-the-paper chance; it had been the product of careful choice. Over the years, there had been various alternatives considered: Lionel, Reginald, Arnold: each rejected for being too old-fashioned. Robert, Richard, Luke, and Laurence had been amongst those to make the mid-term list, which was eventually whittled-down to a final trio: George, heavily favoured for its Britishness, being associated with six former kings and a patron saint. Then, there was Andrew: again patronal and exhibiting a solidity born of its evenly matched syllables. Finally, Jeremy: modern, musical, and little-chosen by other Chinese families seeking to Anglicise their sons' identities. Thus, "Jeremy" it became.

Both his father and his mother used non-Chinese names, also: Gerald and Geraldine. "Gerald" had been acquired at the age of 16, when he had taken the, then, comparatively unusual decision to register in the Sixth Form of an English school, in order to study for his Advanced School Certificate, with the intention of securing a place at a British university. It had been less the product of selection and more akin to the manner in which Oliver Twist had acquired his, at The Workhouse: the next in an alphabetical list. This list was administered by an Imperial Civil Servant when Malaysia, itself, was known by another name. A tweed-suited, toothbrush-moustachioed bureaucrat had also recommended the school to which Gerald should apply. The method of recommendation had been the same as that which had produced the forename. It could have been Eastbourne, or

Epsom, or Eton but the book had not been open at 'E'. "The book", in fact, was arranged both alphabetically and by region. On the day of Gerald's visit, 'N' was on offer. 'N' for Northamptonshire, for Northumberland, for Norfolk.

There were (and there remain) a number of renowned schools in Norfolk. Fothergill's was not one of them. However, as the recently re-named Gerald perched nervously and uncomfortably on the edge of the supple but scarred leather upholstery of the chair to which he had been directed, his fate was fixed. A thick and hairy index finger paused in its journey down the column of entries. "Ah ha, *Fothergill's*; that's the place for you, young man. I was up at the varsity with Archie. Fothergill. Crafty leg-break man, as I recall; very whippy wrist, you know!" The appropriate form was produced, completed, signed and counter-signed, placed in an envelope, sealed, stamped, and dropped into the *out* tray. "Consider it settled, m'boy." A fleshy right hand grasped Gerald's much smaller, finer-boned one, suffocating it. The left hand, simultaneously, was placed in the small of Gerald's back, as he was propelled towards the door with the words, "All the best, m'boy; Archie Fothergill will see you straight, you mark my words, now," which saw him through it and into the corridor beyond.

Geraldine had been Cho-Yu until she had accepted Gerald's proposal of marriage, when she was in her mid-twenties. It was, of course, *his* suggestion. He considered the feminine form of his own name to exhibit British wit; it also established a sense of proprietorship. Over the years, Gerald, had developed a complex personality: an undoubted Anglophile, he had, also, a very conservative Chinese cultural outlook. Geraldine had never travelled abroad until their marriage but she was a well-educated, widely-read, naturally intelligent woman, who was keen to embrace new experiences. She accepted the proposed change of name, not with any degree of servility but as an adventure. To her mind, it developed rather than diminished her. Cho-Yu had not been discarded and replaced by Geraldine; rather she had become, Cho-Yu, Geraldine. An unmarried woman had become a wife, who anticipated becoming a mother and a grandmother. A singular Chinese identity had been expanded into a richer Anglo-Chinese duality.

As well as sharing forms of the same name, Gerald and Geraldine shared a difficulty with its pronunciation: the dominant *r*. Even Gerald's English school and university years had failed to enable him to master the upward curve of the tongue which is required to capture the rounded resonance of his name's central letter. Stubbornly, the tip of his tongue refused to flex, thus transposing *r* into *l*. Geraldine had not been as exposed to native English speakers as her husband and, thus, whilst fluent in her vocabulary and sound in her grammar, she was even more halting in her pronunciation. Especially of her new name. It was for both of them a frustration. It was also the guiding principle behind their selection of an English name for little Hong-Chun, who would receive his first lessons in English from a native speaker and who, thus, would be able to pronounce his name, with impeccable accuracy.

This was a project especially dear to Gerald's heart. His tied tongue had been exposed to English ears at school. Neither Mr. Fothergill nor his charges had been sympathetic towards their 16 year old "visitor from the Orient", as the Headmaster described him. Indeed, they had exercised ridicule so caustic that Gerald, Anglophile though he may well be in so many ways, would never fully recover from the wounds to his dignity. Moreover, he was determined that no child of his would suffer such humiliation for the mere inversion of two simple sounds.

Gerald had been surprised by the speed with which Mr. Fothergill responded to his application. The envelope was impressive: a weight heavier than paper, yet lighter than card; of a colour richer than white yet not quite cream. On its reverse side, embossed in blue-black, raised copperplate, was: *Archibald McPhearson Fothergill, MA (Oxon.)* and, centred beneath: *Headmaster & Proprietor, Fothergill's School.* Gerald, anxious that he had been rejected, took a paper-knife to the envelope, which he carefully sawed open. Within, was a sheet of paper, marginally and judiciously lighter than the envelope but of matching colour and quality and with the same inscription. Then followed, handwritten and in an impressive black, gothic script:

Dear Chan,

I am, today, in receipt of an application purporting to be from you and countersigned by a man in whom I trust sufficiently not to doubt your veracity.

Here, at Fothergill's, we enjoy a full register of scholars. However, I am minded to accept you as an additional member. Should you remain serious in your intent, speed is of the essence, as the start of the Michaelmas Term is but two-weeks from this day. Quintessential to your securing a place will be the lodging of two terms of fees within the School's account, prior to the first day of term and at your very earliest convenience. Kindly make the necessary arrangements. Other details, such as guardianship during the vacations, etc., etc., may be attended to at a later date.

I shall instruct my bankers to keep me informed and I anticipate your arrival forthwith.

Yours sincerely,

A.McP.Fothergill.

Fothergill's.

Gerald had been sufficiently serious in his intentions to have put in place all the necessary financial arrangements, having discussed them at length with his father. Not that he was an indulged child. His father, who had founded a business which he intended Gerald to succeed him in, shared his son's enthusiasm for Western education. This was an entirely utilitarian enthusiasm on the father's part. Technical advances were being developed in the West a knowledge of which would be of enormous benefit to his business. Funds were transferred into the Fothergill's account. Bookings were secured. Gerald packed and departed for London.

It had taken him some considerable amount of map-work to locate the rural backwater in which Fothergill's was located. It was nowhere near Norwich nor, indeed, close to Kings Lynn. Neither a town, nor a village, perhaps 'hamlet' would be the most appropriate term to describe the unnamed huddle of houses amongst which the school's address indicated it to be numbered. Enquiries in London concerning the most convenient route he might take directed Gerald as far as Kings Lynn, where it was suggested he should draw upon more local knowledge. Public transport as far as Sandringham was available but, once there, further links were not in evidence. A passing farmer agreed to divert his cart to Fothergill's, if Gerald would "see oi, roight, boy" – a point made comprehendible only through animated, thumb-and-fingers rubbing sign language. An agreement was reached and thus it was that Gerald finally arrived at Fothergill's, the largest of a small group of houses to be found at the end of a rutted track. Although the largest building, it was no mansion. Mr. Fothergill's letter had referred to "a full register of scholars"; this building comprised but two storeys and no more than ten rooms. It appeared that Fothergill's may, indeed, prove to be an exclusive establishment!

From his researches into English domestic architecture, Gerald concluded that the building had once been a farmhouse and that the others must have been formerly occupied by farm-workers. It was probably late eighteenth century in origin, with both Regency and Victorian additions. Constructed of red brick and slate with sash windows, mullions, and heavy wooden doors, it exhibited what modern Estate Agents might call "rustic charm" but which, even on a sunny mid-September afternoon, exuded neglect. None of the buildings was derelict but none exhibited pride of ownership. They would have benefitted from some re-pointing and re-decoration. Roses climbing up the walls had not been pruned for years and, thus, lengths of bare, woody stems sprouted new but straggly growth near to the guttering, whilst the earth out of which they grew lacked both tilth and other plants. Fothergill's did not set out to impress its clientele.

Whilst he recognised that he had arrived a day before the start of term, Gerald had anticipated a greater sense of bustle and preparation than the seemingly deserted torpor with which he was faced. However, beside the main door, he noticed a heavy iron chain and bell-pull. Hesitantly, he wrapped his slender fingers around the bulbous metal and tugged.

Whilst *he* had heard nothing, evidently a bell had sounded within, for he detected a heavy-footed clomping up an invisible staircase. In addition to the two storeys, there must be a basement. Eventually, the door was opened and a woman of immense bulk filled the space created. Attempting to recover her breath, following her ascent of the stairs, prevented her from saying anything, as she wheezed, and blew, and coughed, and cleared clots of catarrh from her chest. Having been taught that it was rude to stare at strangers, Gerald felt an urgent need to converse but he could generate nothing more articulate than a faltering, "I'm Chan." Nervousness increased Gerald's faulty pronunciation and his particular *l/r* difficulty, especially. "Gelled Chan. Preased meet you."

The woman's heaving bosom suddenly became motionless. "Ay?" was her own and only staccato contribution.

"Gelled Chan. Maraya."

"You'll 'av to speak English, boy. Oi never been further'n Lynn."

"Chan. *Chan. Gelled Chan*," Gerald responded with increasing desperation.

"Cha, cha, cha-cha cha! Oi've 'eard'n on the woirless but oi ant suited to'n."

"Who is it, Maud?" Another voice turned the duet of confused counterpoint into a trio. A male voice, chiselled and educated.

"Ferrin fellah, Sir. Shall oi let'n in?"

"Yes, yes, do." And, at last, the impasse was over, as the human barricade turned sideways, creating space sufficient for Gerald to enter.

Directed by a podgy finger attached to a fleshy hand at the end of a fat arm made muscular by much kneading (for Maud transpired to be the cook) Gerald knocked at the open study door of his new Headmaster. "No need to knock, Chan; not when the door is ajar. Door closed: knock and enter; door ajar: simply enter and await a response. That's our way, Chan."

"Thank you," Gerald replied.

"Thank you, *Sir*, if you don't mind! You Chan; me Sir. You follow?"

"Yes, Sir. Thank you, Sir. I am indebted for advice, Sir, ..."

"Hold it there, Chan!" Mr. Fothergill intercepted any chance of Gerald's response developing further. "One Sir per statement will quite suffice. More might be considered to be ingratiating. Do you understand *ingratiating*, Chan?"

"Yes, Sir. Ingratiating, Sir: sycophancy, fawning, false pleasantry, Sir."

"Very good, Chan. Vocabulary exemplary; slow to embrace new ideas; pronunciation accented-verging-upon-the-comical – *that* we shall work upon. Splendid!" Mr. Fothergill's style of delivery resembled a vocalised memo-to-self. The rhythm of his spoken prose was heavily punctuated with hyphens and semi-colons. Were Gerald yet to have acquired English impishness, he may have mused that it, too, was 'verging-upon-the-comical'.

"So, Chan, welcome to Fothergill's. You are, of course, a day early but with two terms' fees secured, that is acceptable. Not that Cook has been forewarned of early culinary requirements for pupils. Still, I dare say that your meagre frame betokens a preference for light repasts. *Maud*!" His observation had been pursued by a bellow so loud that Gerald found it to be quite alarming. Once again, he heard the creaking of aged staircase steps, whalebone corset, and arthritic knees, in concert with a respiratory system akin to punctured bellows. At last, Maud's magnificent bulk invaded the Headmaster's study. "Allow me to introduce you. Maud : Chan; Chan : Maud, whom *you* shall refer to as Cook. One extra for supper, this evening, please, Maud. Thank you; that will be all." Gerald noted a hint of malice in Maud's expression and he wondered whether this had been generated by his early arrival or her required ascent of the staircase for so brief an interview. "Now, Chan, to business. You shall room with Urquart and Trevellyan. Splendid fellows, both. Neither destined for the varsity but as sound an opening pair as any eleven could hope for. Both hale from your part of the world. Urquart's people are in Ceylon; the Trevellyans do business on The Bund." Whatever Mr. Fothergill's academic discipline might be, evidently it was not Geography; Gerald recognised little common ground between Kuala Lumpur, Colombo, and Shanghai other than all being well to the east of Norfolk.

Fothergill's brusque manner and clipped speech were reflected in his style of dress. A three-piece suit woven from thick, heavy tweed; detachable, starched collar, uncomfortably tight-fitting; club tie; highly-polished brown brogues with an additional layer of sole, increasing their inelegant solidity. Like his university contemporary, thousands of miles away in the Far Eastern Education Service, he sported a tooth-brush moustache, closely cropped, but a face otherwise scraped, clean-shaven, and shiny. His natural athleticism glowed in high-coloured cheeks and confirmed itself in the broad-shouldered, barrel-chested, lean-limbed, six foot frame. This was a body nourished by good, plain cooking, fresh air, and exercise. It had never been subjected to excess, nor to indulgence.

As Fothergill directed his attention to lists and forms and documents pertaining to Gerald's formal registration at the school, the boy's was directed to the trappings of his Headmaster's private study. Spy prints of cricketing heroes adorned the walls. They were arranged symmetrically and with absolute precision, in measured order. A floor-to-ceiling recess housed book shelves. Volumes of *Wisden* occupied the top two, followed by bound volumes of *The Cricketer*. Then came books devoted to golf, hill-walking, and fly-fishing. Baden-Powell's *Scouting For Boys* rubbed shoulders with *The Book of Common Prayer*; then came a sequence of novels by John Buchan, Erskine Childers, 'Sapper', P.C. Wren, and Dornford Yates. Alphabetical-by-author was the system of order, within associated subject matter. Fothergill's taste in reading, like his appearance, was indisputably 'healthy'.

The walls and ceiling of the study were painted an especially crisp tone of white; the curtains were long swathes of earth-coloured twill, not dissimilar to Fothergill's suit; the floor was a combination of shining lengths of timber, tongue-and-grooved, with a centrally positioned carpet of mingled heather hues. The desk at which Fothergill sat was mahogany (with matching carver chair) and a firmly-stuffed leather settee was placed before it. Two further leather chairs, matching each other but not the settee, completed the equilateral triangle of comfortable seating, whilst a selection of rail-backed dining chairs had been placed against walls at various (possibly strategic) points. Between the desk and the settee was an occasional table, upon which had been placed copies of *Country Life* and *The Illustrated London News*. A cut-glass sherry decanter, sitting on a silver salver and surrounded by matching glasses rested upon the narrow central section of a drop-leaved table, positioned within the bay window area, the window, itself, offering a view over the grounds, outside. Having not been invited to sit, Gerald allowed himself to absorb these details, making as little movement as observation permitted. Eventually, Fothergill rose from his desk. "Time-table, weekly routine, regulations, punishments for disobeying them, school list." As each of these items was announced, the Headmaster handed his new pupil the relevant sheet of paper. "That should keep you going for the time being. I'll take you to your room. You can unpack and then read through this little lot. Supper is at 6.45 prompt. There will be a gong. Off we go, now!" And, setting a brisk pace, Fothergill swept out of his study, carrying Gerald in his wake.

The Mistaken Mackintosh.

Jeremy was well aware that his father had been one of the earliest overseas pupils to have ventured into the English education system. Indeed, he had been regaled with stories of those times by Gerald, throughout his childhood. Inevitably, these stories had become coloured with nostalgia, tinged with time-honed humour, and embroidered in the telling and re-telling. Some had become family classics. "Dad, dad, tell us the one about the raincoat!" became an oft repeated request. And so, with feigned reluctance and exaggerated protestation, Gerald would settle to his task.

Fothergill's, as he had realised upon his arrival, was not a school out of the top drawer. Certainly, it was not of the calibre of those colleges beginning with 'E' that he may just as fortuitously have been directed towards. Fothergill's, correctly defined, was "a private school". This means that it was more a small-time money-spinner for its proprietor than an educational institution. At the time, such establishments were subject to no government scrutiny, standardisation, nor expectation. Having left university, Archie Fothergill had hoped to spend his time playing cricket. However, as a Gentleman, rather than a Player, he did not have the financial independence to fund his preferred occupation. As a result, he came to use a small inheritance to purchase a remote and deserted Norfolk farmhouse with associated dependent buildings. Unable to practise his passion, he decided to teach others to play the noble game. But this was decades before the existence of Sports' Academies and so he needed a cover. Thus it was that Fothergill's came into being.

As the school gradually established itself - drawing its pupils mainly from the families of Archie's university acquaintances: non-cerebral boys whom their fathers had failed to secure places for amongst the more cached establishments - it acquired the patina of eccentricity associated with them. Both because he was new and because he had been accepted as a late addition to the regular clientele, (of course, a cash-flow crisis had prompted his swift acceptance) Gerald was ignorant both of the school's foundation and of its *raison d'etre*. He was also ignorant of its foibles.

As the mild mid-September day upon which he had made his early arrival gave way to a crisp Autumn and then to the damp, foggy days of November, Gerald felt the cold more than most. He decided to purchase what was, at that time, rather quaintly known as a mackintosh. This would provide an extra layer of clothing and protection against the rain, driven-in remorselessly by on-shore north-easterly winds characteristic of the region. His room-mates, Urquart and Trevellyan, took an unusual interest in this decision, first made known to them by Gerald's seeking advice as to where he might purchase such an article.

Although Fothergill's suggestion that their home addresses would make them natural companions had proven to be over-fanciful, Urquart and Trevellyan rubbed along reasonably well with Gerald. They were likeable enough in their way. Happiest on The Square or in The Nets, during the summer, and in The Gym or on The Rugger Pitch in winter, they spent little time in the room they shared with Gerald. They were with him in the evenings, mainly, struggling with their Prep. This engendered a degree of affability for, once they had struggled for long enough (giving their companion time to work his way through the tasks he had been set) Gerald was able to do all their Maths and Science work for them. Given his superb vocabulary, he was even able to help them with their English and History essays. As neither of them had any facility for foreign languages, which they had abandoned as early as possible, this potential pitfall was avoided. He kept them out of Detention and, thus, they accepted him, even if it could not truthfully be said that they befriended him. Urquart and Trevellyan were too shallow for either friendship or enmity. However, "a wheeze" was well within their orbit of activity.

Thus, when Gerald raised the question of purchasing a mackintosh, his room-mates exhibited unwonted enthusiasm for such a comparatively domestic issue. Certainly, they felt, Gerald would be wise to make the purchase. Given the encroaching winter, with its rain, day after day, until the arrival of snow, and then the increasingly bitter winds blowing off the North Sea with neither hills, nor forests, nor housing between the coast and Fothergill's to reduce its force, they could not urge him more strongly to take a Saturday Exeat in pursuit of the garment.

Accordingly, Gerald sought permission to meet "an additional clothing requirement". A chit was signed and a taxi ordered. Whilst, ordinarily, Saturday afternoons were sacrosanct at Fothergill's - it was match time – Gerald's prowess at Rugby had proven to be of little worth to the XV. In essence, he was surplus to requirement (although the Headmaster still held-out hope for Hockey and Cricket, "as the Academic Year unfolds." Gerald still puzzled over Fothergill's conception of an *academic* year!) When he had made his bid for a Saturday Exeat chit, he had not been required to specify his needs. He had merely explained that he had come to recognise that he had not brought with him all the clothing he needed and that, thus, he needed to make a purchase. His mind preoccupied with the forthcoming home fixtures, Fothergill had merely scrawled "additional clothing" in the log and dismissed Gerald with a reminder not to be late and not to forget to sign the Gate List, upon return. "Actually, Chan," he called after the retreating figure, "just pop-in and let me know you're safely returned."

The nearest High Street was in a town several miles away and the taxi driver had a number of other fares booked for the afternoon. Gerald told him by what time he must return to school and a time to be collected from the central square, several hours later, was agreed. This had been his first period away from Fothergill's since his arrival and he enjoyed the un-timetabled hours between his two taxi journeys, enormously. Ordinarily, a Saturday afternoon found him dutifully treading the touchline in support of the home team. Treading it to keep warm, rather than out of absorbed involvement in the proceedings, which he found bewildering at best, barbaric even, at times. His purchase secured, he luxuriated, both in the additional warmth the garment offered and in the ensuing idle hours of window gazing, book-shop browsing, coffee-sipping, and cake-sampling. Just to sit and watch the passing crowd, busily involved in a whole range of individual projects, added to the glow of contentment he felt. The time sped swiftly by and the chiming of a clock in the central square prompted him to pay his bill and to make his way to the agreed meeting point, where he found the taxi driver good to his word and waiting. It had been a fraught-free afternoon. Not even the prospect of returning to Fothergill's blighted his sense of untrammelled pleasure.

Mr. Fothergill's afternoon had been less delightful. The XV had been well-and-truly trounced. It had been, Fothergill had fulminated to his so-called Head Coach (the singular P.E. Instructor employed by the school), "A travesty, an absolute travesty of the game. Incompetent fumbling; inept passing; gutless tackling; no notion of defensive play, let alone an iota of gumption in attack! Shameful. Utterly-bloody-shameful!" And, with that, he had retired to his study to sulk.

That had been three hours before Gerald's taxi eased itself down the rutted track that announced his return to the school. He paid the friendly driver, who left with a cheery, "Back to the grindstone then, young man. All the best, now." Gerald entered through the heavy, creaking door and went straight to the gate list, which he signed in order to confirm his return. He started to make his way towards the room he shared with Urquart and Trevellyan, in order to model his mackintosh. Then he suddenly remembered Fothergill's afterthought: "... just pop-in and let me know you're safely returned." Thus, he changed direction and made his way to the Headmaster's Study. The door being shut, he knocked and entered.

Private, small-time, insignificant school though Fothergill's, in truth, was, Archie Fothergill had accreted to it arcane traditions beloved of the Major Public Schools. Utilitarian objects had names not to be found in *The Oxford Dictionary*: rooms were *sets*; desks were *dens*; lavatories were *backs*. A system of "capping" operated within the school precincts. This was a form of greeting between pupils and staff. The pupil should raise the right index finger to his brow, upon encountering a teacher, who would reciprocate. Breaks within term-time were lent Latin epithets, as were three boys who shared a name: Raleigh *Ma.*,

Mi., and *Min.*, for example. There had even been developed a form of Fothergill's patois (based upon that at Repton, itself possibly borrowed from Eton.) Matron was *The Nagger*; the Groundsman was *The Digger*; the school's accountant (Forthergill's did not run to a Bursar) was *The Adder*. It took time for a newly arrived pupil to acquire a comprehensive knowledge of this deliberate mystique. Had Gerald gone straight to his room, he would have had an eleventh hour reprieve from what was about to take place. Urquart and Trevellyan were not malicious enough to allow their jape to develop into its fullest consequence. But, dutiful as ever, Gerald halted and then re-directed his steps, which is why he knocked upon Fothergill's study door and entered, dressed in his mackintosh, without Urquart and Trevellyan's vital clarification.

"So, Chan, what's all this to do with?" snapped the still-smarting Fothergill.

"Safely back, Sir," responded Gerald.

"And what have you been up to, young man?"

"Saturday Exeat, Sir."

"Abused, I presume. Oh well, let's get it over with. Collect the chair!"

"Sir?"

"Collect the chair, Chan! No shilly-shallying! Best done and dealt!"

"Sir?" repeated the bewildered Gerald. He understood that Fothergill was angry with him but he did not understand why.

"Chair, Chan: *collect it!*" Not only did he raise his voice for emphasis but he transformed the phrase into a sequence of syllables more than it was actually composed of, for clarity.

Fothergill's finger was pointing at a particular and peculiar chair, placed in a corner of the room. Its back had a triangular structure, but a regulation square seat, and it was especially designed to sit, snugly and seldom noticed, in a corner.

Gerald approached the chair, picked it up, and turned around for further explanation. "Centre of the room, Chan; grip its arms and take your medicine!"

Very slowly but with an increasing clarity, Gerald began to understand what was taking place. He was to be thrashed! "But, but, but, Sir," he spluttered.

"But me no buts, Chan, as the Bard would have it. Bend over." And before he could utter another word, Gerald found himself gripping the arms of the chair, bending over, his head buried within the folds of his mackintosh, which Fothergill had uplifted and re-draped.

Four stinging blows to his buttocks in quick succession were followed by, "Right you are, Chan. Stand up. Return the chair and sign the book." Motivated by a combination of pain, outrage, and confusion, Gerald moved like a sleepwalker. He replaced the chair in its allotted corner and approached Fothergill's desk, upon which a leather-bound ledger was opened and onto a page of which Fothergill was writing information. The page had been divided into neatly headed columns: *Name*; *Date*; *Offence*; *Punishment*; *Signature*; *HM Initials*. Columns 1, 2, 4 and 6 had now been filled-in. Fothergill handed Gerald the pen. "Complete the details, if you would be so kind, Chan, and then sign." Still too numbed to weep or even to protest, Gerald looked blankly at Fothergill. What was he to write? "Come along, Chan. You're no simpleton. Come clean; fill-in the detail of your offence, sign, and then get yourself off to the showers. Best thing by far for a blackened backside: plenty of hot water!" Fothergill rasped.

After an age of silence, Gerald ventured with his utmost courtesy, "But, Sir, I have committed no offence."

"Nonsense, boy! Why else should you have appeared before me, thus?" And his right hand gestured towards Gerald, still enwrapped in his mackintosh. *"Get on with it and then get out!"*

What Urquart and Trevellyan would, eventually, have revealed to him, had he gone straight back to their room upon returning from his shopping expedition was another exemplum of Fothergill's lore: a boy in a mackintosh presenting himself to the Headmaster was code for: "I have offended and require to be punished."

The matter was never mentioned again. Not verbally. Not in any written report nor reference. It was as if it had never taken place. Until, that is, Jeremy was old enough to hear his father's now-comedic version, many

years later.

Against All Odds.

The remainder of Gerald's time at Fothergill's ran fairly free from incident. As part of what the British excuse as banter, he had to endure unkind comments concerning his accented pronunciation (the notorious *l/r* interchange prompting the most frequent ribaldry) and reprises of the mistaken mackintosh narrative became embedded within the weft and woof of school history. Urquart and Trevellyan remained his room-mates, throughout, as they prepared for their lives as a Minor Counties Cricket and Rugby representative and a Small Market Town Estate Agent.

Access to academic expertise remained remote but a combination of natural intelligence, Chinese self-discipline, and increasing expectations from home prompted Gerald to pursue his original intention of securing British university entrance. This, itself, was an exercise in logistical gymnastics.

Understandably, both Gerald and Archie. Fothergill gave one another a wide berth. Faux-enthusiasm shaped the Headmaster's greetings when the building's narrow corridors forced them to acknowledge one another's presence: "Morning, Chan; how goes it? Splendid, splendid. Carry on, m'boy!" Impeccable (if inscrutable) courtesy coloured Gerald's responses: "Good morning, Sir. I am well, thank you, Sir. Good day to you, Sir." Towards the end of his first year, Gerald received a summons to the Headmagisterial presence. Hesitantly, he made his way to Fothergill's study. He knocked. He entered.

"Ah, Chan. Take a pew." Carefully avoiding the beating chair, Gerald selected one of the peripherally placed seats, inching it into the room's interior. "Had a letter from your father, Chan. Thought we should chat. It appears that you aspire towards Higher Education.   The Varsity."   With economy of responsiveness, Gerald replied,

"Yes, Sir."

"And,........................... ."

"Yes, Sir?"

"Well? ...."

Any capacity these two had ever had to conduct a purposeful conversation appeared to have vanished. "What are you minded to read?"

"My father would like me to acquire advanced knowledge of Chemical Engineering, Sir."

"Chemical Engineering, eh?" Whatever source of intellectual curiosity may once have motivated Fothergill's mental faculties, 'Stinks' was most certainly not it. He knew absolutely nothing about it, whatsoever. Nor, for that matter, did he wish to. "Very, ...," again the hiatus seemed likely to develop into prolonged silence. "Very," he negotiated a second approach; "practical."

"Yes, Sir."

"Very utilitarian. D'ya know 'utilitarian', Chan?"

"Utilitarian; yes, Sir: put to good purpose, Sir."

"Quite, Chan. Quite." A ruminative pause followed. Then: "And where, Chan, do you propose to read Chemical Engineering?" An inescapable redolence of distastefulness accompanied the phrase, as if there were something not quite respectable about it. Something not exactly 'Fothergill's'.

"Manchester, Sir."

"Manchester?" This was no mere interrogative. There was a hint of disbelief, a tinge of surprise that resonated doubt. Whether Fothergill was uncertain as to the geographical location of Manchester, or unaware that a university was to be found there, or unsure whether Chemical Engineering could be studied at it, was not clear. But the way in which he enunciated that one word indicated the undermining of some previously rock-solid foundation. "Manchester," he repeated, attempting to regain lost ground by eradicating any tone of uncertainty from his intonation.

"Yes, Sir." Whether deliberately or not, Gerald was not helping to bring any degree of ease into this exchange.

Not only was this a topic of conversation beyond Fothergill's reach, he had been unnerved ever since opening and reading Mr. Chan's letter. Even he had to acknowledge (albeit privately and alone,) that university admission was not one of his school's strong points. Over the years, there had been the occasional entrant into his old Oxford College to read Forestry, as an excuse for acquiring a Blue or two, but otherwise that particular area of scholarship had become pretty well untilled earth. Other than dropping a line to his increasingly aged Tutor, or the old Bursar, recommending a first-rate sportsman, Fothergill had had little or nothing to do with directing pupils to university. To him, it was a discipline as arcane as Sanscrit! But there was no avoiding the issue. Mr. Chan's letter had been quite explicit: *"Please to tell by returning postal communication, procedure involved."* the letter had concluded.

As if his father's request and Fothergill's discomfort had been psychically transmitted into Gerald's brain, the boy asked, "When do I need to apply, Sir?" When, indeed?!

"Not immediately," Fothergill retorted with dissembling authority.

"Before the end of the year, Sir? Or will I have the Summer Holiday for further debate with my father?" Crucial questions, both of these, and equally crucial was it for Fothergill to offer accurate replies.

"The, er, the *provincial universities*," he gave the phrase as much *hauteur* as he could manage, in order to denigrate Gerald's ambition to the maximum, "have never adopted as clear a path towards securing places as our more ancient seats of learning. Indeed, quite understandably, not having had the centuries of practice and experience behind them, tinkering with their system has become quite characteristic and it has been several years since a scholar from Fothergill's has looked to, er, to *Manchester* to become his *alma mater*." With mounting confidence, or its devised counterfeit, Fothergill captured the high ground of superiority and superciliousness. "So, Chan, m'boy, you leave it with me and I shall put out some feelers for you. Very good; off you go. No point in wasting time on speculation that could be so much more profitably spent upon developing and securing the knowledge you will require to exhibit in the examinations, is there, now?!" For the one, this was a metaphorical exit strategy;

for the other, it was literally so. Gerald rose, replaced the chair against a wall, and retreated. Fothergill took pen and paper, in order to write a letter to Manchester University, enquiring about their current entry procedures. After all, Mr. Chan's letter had requested a response "by returning postal communication", damn him to blazes!

Little in the way of tuition or guidance was no impediment to a motivated and dedicated Chinese student. It would have taken much more than a negligent school to fell Gerald's ambitions. The appropriate application procedure was pursued with success; the curriculum was absorbed; the grades were attained and Gerald bad farewell to Fothergill's, as he embarked upon the next phase of his life. Three years of diligent study led to his acquiring a good degree and the up-to-date technological expertise desired by his father. His brief but significant relocation in the West had equipped him with an admiration for British finesse and a shrewd suspicion of British aplomb. He felt that his native seriousness of purpose, matched with an acquired carapace of false self-deprecation, would arm him to succeed in the world of business he planned to make his own. As with so much else, Gerald's anticipations proved to be finely judged.

Adjustments.

Jeremy had come to understand that his parents embraced dual identities. With their Chinese friends and business associates, they used their Chinese names and spoke Mandarin; with Europeans, they insisted upon their Western identities and their own brand of accented English. With this, he was totally at ease. Happy to be called Hong-Chun or Jeremy, he was equally happy to speak in Mandarin or in English; he had a facility with both languages.

Thus, when Gerald and Geraldine began to speak about his moving into the British education system, Jeremy felt no fear. Fothergill's, he knew, had collapsed years before and his father was very much in the know about the current educational scene in Britain. Just as his name had been carefully considered and selected, so too was his new school.

Like so many Independent Boarding Schools, Jeremy's was a Nineteenth Century foundation, constructed, in the main, of red brick and mirroring the architectural spirit of that Neo-Gothic bastion, St. Pancras' Railway Station. Towered and turreted, machicolated, gargoyled, porticoed, and clad in Virginian Creeper, it was a vision of romanticised medi*ae*valism. The grounds, planted a century and a half before Jeremy's arrival, were defined by mature trees: limes and oaks, chestnuts and wellingtonias, cedars, yews, ashes, and *sorbus* of sundry varieties. Not as grand as the designs of Capability Brown nor of Humphrey Repton, these grounds, mixing manicured lawns with expanses of sports' fields, cottage garden planting, coppices, and pottagers, undulating over a gentle gradient, were, indeed, "...

nature methodis'd." Casting his gaze as far as he could, Gerald recalled a rutted Norfolk track, leading to a huddle of nondescript buildings. He felt satisfied. *This* was the genuine article.

The Chans arrived in the U.K. three weeks before Jeremy's first term was due to start. This was in order to avoid unnecessary haste and possible oversights. It enabled them to visit and to acquaint themselves with both the geography of the school and the man who described himself as "the first port of call" - Jeremy's Housemaster.

"Jo San! Jo San! Cantonese, I know; HK not KL but at least I know I've got it wrong, which is to be half-way-there!" Loud in an endearing sort of way; self-deprecating; oozing confidence and generating *bon hommie*, he greeted and welcomed them, as he ushered them through his front door and signalled the direction into his sitting room. "Do flop!" and they sank into comfortable seats, feeling much more at ease than they had anticipated. "I'm Charles Wimpole and whether it be an outbreak of Athlete's Foot or an overwhelming desire to break out of this zariba, I'm your first port of call! Know what a zariba is, Jeremy? Course you don't; why should you? Here you are, look it up!" And a medium-sized dictionary was lobbed exaggeratedly through the air in the boy's direction. "Well caught, Sir! *Z a r i b a*; found it?"

"Yes, sir: 'fenced camp in the Sudan; enclosure for cattle; sheepfold'."

"That's the fellah and what's more we've now probably doubled the percentage of the world's population who know that word! Education, you see, it's magic!" Laughter all-round. Not feigned, sycophantic laughter but genuine chortles of pent-up tension escaping in an easeful rush.

"Anyway, back to names. Mr. & Mrs. Chan, please feel free to address me as Charlie; may I call you Gerald and Geraldine? Convention decrees that *he*" (with pantomime pointing) "must call me 'Sir' - well, to my face, at least! Now, time for a tincture: sherry, gin, wine white or red, beer, lager, shandy. Name your poison."

Gerald at first demurred on behalf of his whole family, saying that they did not want to take-up too much of .... he paused and then fought-off the natural pull of Chinese formality by allowing "Charlie" to pass his lips .... of Charlie's time. "Nonsense!" asserted the Housemaster, rising from his chair, "I'm employed to have too much of my time taken-up! Now then, Geraldine, ladies first!"

This offered Geraldine the rarest, yet most momentarily awkward, of opportunities. Used to agreeing, duplicating, following, she was being asked to lead, to set the tone, to innovate. Here was a chance to crash through the walls of her personal zariba! "White wine would be most welcome," she brazened, feeling the inner energy of a risk now taken with no opportunity to retract.

"White wine, it is; Gerald, what about you? And is a beer for the big fellah permitted?" Whilst his personal taste in wine inclined to white, Gerald was not minded to take-on Geraldine's habitual role of follower and so he elected for red and told Jeremy that, if he would like to try a beer, he may." Within half-an-hour of arriving, new ground had already been broken.

Drinks having been produced, Charlie Wimpole turned to business, providing information, guidance, and documentation. Without asking, he provided top-ups, as he continued, in as natural a manner as if he had been acquainted with this trio for years. Then it was time to look around the House and the School Campus before returning to his sitting room, where a final round was served, as questions were posed and answered. The Chans went on their way, feeling old-hands. Jeremy could not wait for the days to pass and for term to start.

And when it did start, he was not disappointed.

A Duck To Water.

Whilst there were other pupils from overseas, both in his House and in the School, Jeremy was the only one within his particular group of immediate peers. This might have resulted in a degree of isolation but, in fact, it integrated him even better than his gregarious nature would have ensured, anyway. Partly, this was the result of his extraordinary spoken English. Hear his voice without looking to see who was speaking and it would be assumed to be that of an English boy; re-embody the voice and the effect was quite dislocating. Those with whom he rubbed shoulders found this to be fascinating, at first, and then, as they became used to the novelty, it seemed as if the thousands of geographic miles and of counter-cultural years that separated him from them did not exist. To them, he became merely their mate, 'Jezza'.

Without question, he was extremely bright, academically, and he had a genuinely enquiring intellect. He enjoyed his lessons; even more, he enjoyed accomplishing the work he was set and extending his research well beyond its bounds. And yet, he was never chained to his desk. Come the bell which signalled the end of evening Prep., and he was as ready as anyone else to play table-tennis, watch T.V., listen to music, flop and talk football. He was an efficient and effective worker, who systematically sliced through the set tasks and then turned his attention to wider, more advanced, issues. This enabled him to cover much more ground than his friends, without compromising his capacity for seeming normality.

Before his arrival at the school, he had generated a genuine interest in English football and he had embraced Accrington Stanley as 'his' team. How easy it would have been to adopt Man. U. or Chelsea, 'the Gunners', Spurs, or 'Toon'. Magic though there was to be discerned in these teams, it did not equate with the allure of Accrington Stanley – a team of two words, five syllables, accentuated consonants, and, most significantly for Jeremy, an *r* and an *l*. He rolled the name around his mouth, like a premier cru, releasing it slowly, almost salaciously, lending it a luxuriance quite at odds with the club's Mancunian origins. He was well-versed in the team's history; in its roll-call of players, past and present; in its moments of glory and its troughs of disappointment. He could rehearse phases of play in recent matches with a recall so vivid that it was as if he were commentating upon tele-replay in his brain. As he acquired a knowledge of British football pundits, he was able to put his innate talent for mimicry to comic effect and, thereby, to turn his enthusiasm into a party-piece that never failed to please an ever-increasing body of admirers.

Academic though he was, football for Jeremy was no mere screen-and-paper activity. He was a player. Here, once again, he occupied highly individualistic ground. Ask the average overseas' pupil what his favoured football position is and he is likely to assert "the number 7 shirt". Sometimes the assertion is sincere, sometimes it is the product of carefully researched popularity, designed to avoid revealing an ignorance or lack of interest that would be socially restricting. Jeremy was a Goalkeeper. Bigger than his father and of a more athletic build, he was nevertheless smaller than the average European. Combining acute senses with agility, however, enabled him to perform with a degree of expertise 'in goal'. He was quick to read an attacking player's game and he employed the anticipatory skills of a chess-player, as much as those of a ball-player, in defending his area. Whilst never a risk-taking exhibitionist, he did enjoy the close spectator focus upon his chosen position and used it to exploit his taste for the bold, the dramatic, the witty. Indeed, there was something of the showman about Jeremy and, like all showmen, his reward was audience response and involvement in his performance.

Such an approach in life can lead to unpopularity. Few like an egoist, even when they proclaim admiration. But Jeremy took care not to transgress in this respect. He was a genuine team member; his loyalty was to the other ten players, first, before promoting his own cause. Indeed, 'took care' suggests a calculation that was, in truth, absent from his game. His was an insouciance devoid of strategy. Be it football or friendships, essays or enterprises, he simply excelled.

Thus, his school years passed with ease and with success. Only the restrictive nature of the British Academic Curriculum presented to him potential discomfort, for there came points at which some subjects must be relinquished, choices must be made, combinations needed to be considered. It was clear that Jeremy was equally able in all academic areas. Thus, as he moved towards the Sixth Form, it was important to be looking several steps ahead, at what career he would like to pursue. Such an innocent word, 'like', and yet, potentially, as corrosive a concept as any defined by far uglier vocabulary.

Letters, faxes, emails, texts, and telephone calls between England and Malaysia, between son and parents, between Charlie Wimpole, Gerald and Geraldine occupied paper, time and cyberspace. Jeremy had made it clear to his Housemaster that, whilst he was not averse to Chemical Engineering (his father's favoured choice of university subject for his son) neither was he overly enthusiastic about it. Similarly, whilst he knew that it had ever been Gerald's intention that a third generation of Chans should guide the family business into the twenty-first century, he did not find the prospect to be overly appealing.

"O.K.," observed Charlie Wimpole, "so where does this leave us? What your father regards to be self-evident is by no means cut-and-dried in your mind. We all know that you *could* follow his lead; the question is would you rather head-off in a different direction? If so, what is that possible direction or, indeed, what are *those* possible *directions*? These are questions that must be answered before any decisions can be taken. Your call, m'boy."

"But it's not my call, is it? I may well have achieved a token Englishness but the fact remains that I'm a Chinaman. Or, rather, that my father is. I'm what a Sociologist would regard as an Educational Paradox: offered a glimpse of paradise to which my peers back home are blind but denied free access to it." His tone was less bitter than it may have been but, without doubt, it conveyed more than a low degree of frustration.

"Powerfully put. And not without a deep vein of truth," noted Charlie, both his voice and his expression revealing the contradictions drawing-up opposing armies within himself. He felt proud of the role he had played in the past three years of Jeremy's total school success. Of course, it was not wholly down to him and it could not have happened at all without Jeremy's extraordinary talents and attitude. But he had, without doubt, facilitated that success and now he was being forced to call into question whether, in fact, 'success' was the right word, at all. Might Jeremy have been better-off staying in Kuala Lumpur; might he have benefited more from being guided by a latter-day Fothergill than by himself? It was not Jeremy, alone, who had questions to answer, conclusions to draw. The warm and comforting sunshine filtering through the open study window was as inappropriate a piece of pathetic fallacy as any author could have devised.

Geraldine.

"*White wine would be wonderful.*" Three years had passed since she had, hesitantly, delivered those five simple and seemingly innocuous words but she had never forgotten them, nor the context out of which they had emerged. "*Ladies first*". Geraldine first. *Her* choice; *her* decision; *her* first ever opportunity to say, in essence, "Take no notice of my husband. If he does not wish to accept your offered hospitality, so be it; let him go without. *I* would like to taste your wine. That's *my* preference." Gerald's subsequent request for red had not escaped her notice. He never chose red; he disliked the tannins that formed the taste-base of red wine; white had always been his selection. It was not that he had disapproved of Geraldine taking a drink but his lead had not been followed; she had not fallen into step with him; she had been made drunk, not by alcohol but by a cultural difference. Charlie Wimpole had regarded her as an individual in her own right; he had failed to pay due regard to other traditions. His drinking red wine was code. Code that had escaped the Englishman's notice but it had not escaped Geraldine's; she had known *exactly* what it meant. Gerald would rather have endured the, to his palate, bitter dryness of red wine than seem to have suggested a willingness to be guided by his wife. By a woman.

Do not make the simplistic assumption that theirs was a marriage in trouble. That would be a Western analysis. This marriage was adamantine and adamantine would it remain. *Never* had the moment been referred to, not even during the hours immediate to their departure from their first encounter with Charlie Wimpole.

There had been no sulking, nor awkward silence; no need to repair damage; no alteration to their habitual co-existence. But those five words had been revelationary. Something that Geraldine had always known but had never acknowledged about herself had been momentarily illuminated. Something that had never occurred to Gerald about his wife had been defined and clarified.

For nearly three years both revelled in the letters that Jeremy wrote to them from school, in the end-of-term reports, in the Headmaster's commendations that their son had earned, in the private messages sent to them by Charlie Wimpole, extolling Jeremy's extraordinary progress, in the cards and letters they received from English families whom Jeremy visited and spent half-terms with. No parents could have been prouder; no greater evidence of their wisdom in sending Jeremy away to school could possibly exist.

Then a *pro forma* had arrived, requiring their signature and authorising Jeremy's choice of A Level subjects. Most pupils were restricted to three but, as an exceptionally gifted academic, Jeremy was permitted to select five. He had used pencil to indicate his selection. This did not betoken uncertainty; it merely made for greater final neatness in the event of change. Maths and Further Maths caused Gerald no concern. The mark of an analytical mind; subjects embracing intellectual purity and practical application. The basis of all good scientific study; essential to engineering of any sub-discipline. It was the remaining three pencilled ticks that triggered the white-water rapids of multi-media correspondence and Jeremy's intensely personal conversation with Charlie Wimpole. Philosophy, Social

Anthropology, and English Literature were totally disassociated from the world of Chemical Engineering.

Dear Son,

Your mother and I have received communication re A Level choices which has caused us much confusion. Perhaps errors in tickings have occurred.

We are happy to see you show interest in Mathematics but we do not understand other possible mistakes.

We copy this to your Housemaster and hope for correct copy to sign by return.

Your parents,

Chan, Gerald ....

Chan, Geraldine ....

Copy: C. Wimpole, Esq., M.A. (Housemaster.)

When Gerald gave his wife the letter to sign against her printed name, she complied. However, she did not comply within her heart.

Geraldine had nothing against the Chan Family business into which Gerald had followed his father. Indeed, she was well aware how comfortable a life-style it had afforded her. Following their marriage, there had been a period when Gerald's father had retained all the financial responsibility, devolving technological direction to his son. This had been ideal. They could settle into their married life without it being eroded by financial worries and extra hours at the office. On the other hand, Gerald was satisfied with his responsibilities and enjoying the application of his university-acquired knowledge to the plant. His hours were regular; the impact upon the business of his introductions was to increase the profit margins; he and Geraldine were soon in a position to buy a much more comfortable property and to feel confident in starting a family. Jeremy's birth had not determined that Geraldine would be devoted to full-time child-minding, for they were wealthy enough to hire help. The business having established so secure a footing, Gerald's father had told his son to nominate a time at which he felt ready to take over the Chairmanship and he would happily step aside. This had duly taken place without any hitches. The Chans: Gerald, Geraldine, and Jeremy, led an almost golden life.

No, it was not antipathy towards the business that prompted Geraldine to side, internally, with her son's subject choices; choices that, evidently, did not lead in the direction of his joining the business. It was her enhanced awareness of the importance of choice in life. Her hand signed the letter that Gerald presented to her but it was a mere mechanical exercise. It did not betoken agreement, let alone assent. It betokened expectation.

So, Where Does This Leave Us?

Inappropriate though it might be, the glorious summer afternoon persisted.

Charlie Wimpole and Jeremy maintained the positions they had held when their conversation had reached its impasse. Each wished to help the other forwards; neither could see an obvious route to take.

"O.K.," said Charlie with resolve, "recognition number 1: there's no 'and they all lived happily ever after' solution to this. Recognition number 2: doing nothing and hoping this whole bloody issue's going to disappear is not an option. Recognition number 3: I'm powerless to *make* anyone in this business *do* anything but I can't avoid causing upset and offence, even if I were to shrug my shoulders and walk away from it. With me, so far?"

"Sorry, Sir."

"A kind thought, Jeremy, but no bloody good to man nor beast! Let's both put our flack-jackets on and break all the rules: 'Tell truth and shame the Devil;/Shame the Devil by telling truth.' Quotation from?"

"Shakespeare, Sir."

"Quite right. Go to the top of the class, that man! Here's another: 'Speak what we feel, not what we ought to say.' Spot a theme?"

"Exercise courage of convictions, come what may?"

"Spot-on! Now, why might Shakespeare repeat this idea through the mouths of characters we find to be attractive?"

"Because, by making such characters voice such opinions, credence, weight, and authority is lent to those opinions."

"You've sat in my classroom for far too bloody long; it's like listening to myself! But *yes*, I *do* believe that to have been Shakespeare's dramatic purpose and technique. And what's more, if English Literature has *any* human function, what-so-bloody-ever, (and I, for one, believe it has) the top man in World Lit. ought to be taken note on! So, cards on the table: is the A Level selection you sent home the one, in an ideal world, you would like to stick with?"

"Yes, Sir."

"And do you have any notion where that particular gallimaufry is likely to take you? You know 'gallimaufry', don't you?"

"Yes, Sir: gallimaufry is a gorgeous word meaning cocktail, or mixture. You taught it to me. Not that it bloody solves anything!" Jeremy's mimicry crept into that final comment; it was accompanied by the flicker of a grin to indicate that he knew he was chancing his arm but that he was not taking liberties. It was his way of signalling that he had stopped feeling sorry for himself and that he was up for finalisation - even if that, paradoxically, did not embrace resolution. He loved the high-wire acrobatics of the English language. "Ideal scenario: Maths and Philosophy at Oxford or Cambridge; a First; transfer to the Ivy League in The States, PhD, post-Doctoral research and a life-time in academe. Is that arrogant? What my father does not understand is that he's bred a weirdo and weirdos just don't fit into neat pre-packaged programmes."

"Well, that's the Devil shamed, then! Arrogant? Certainly not; 'ideal scenario' precludes arrogance - plus the total viability of your proposition. So: next move: CW sells outlandish game-plan to the parents Chan - easy!"

"I wouldn't say 'parents' Chan, myself, Sir. I'm sure my mother will be cool. Problem is, she doesn't count. I expect she's wracked with guilt because I've inherited all her rebel genes. I'd love to know where she got them from! But, hey, I've gone too far. Shakespeare's all very well but he can lead you astray!"

"Discuss ferociously! O.K. progress made. Well done. I'll write, outlining the positives and avoiding any reference to the family business and its future. But I must ask you to consider one question: what if the answer is '*NO*' ?"

Jeremy rose from his chair, thanked Mr. Wimpole for his time, for his patience, for his wisdom and for his guidance. Then he left the room. Charlie's last question had not been answered.

In response to his promised letter, he received the following reply:

Dear Mr. Charlie,

It is troublesome of Jeremy to take up so much of your time but Geraldine and I are grateful for your consideration.

We have spent time with Jeremy on skype, this weekend, and are happy to report resolution to uncertainties re A Level subject choices.   He will study Maths, Further Maths, Physics, Chemistry, and Biology.

Our good wishes, as always.

Chan, Gerald & Geraldine.

Copies: Headmaster.

Jeremy Chan.

There was never any further discussion. Charlie's one attempt to check-out Jeremy's feelings was met with a witty, courteous rebuff, signalling no wish to pursue the matter. Not even his two closest friends, Harry and Tom., ever managed to penetrate his cultural carapace to discover his true feelings about the matter.

He won a scholarship to Cambridge to read Chemical Engineering, which he secured by passing all five of his A Levels with the highest marks in the country for each and, thus, his time at school came to an end.

A Display Of Pyrotechnics.

Jeremy's arrival at Cambridge began much as his time at school had ended. Generally regarded as brilliant, he excelled at everything he turned his mind and time to. He retained his passion for football and, in his second year, he played for the Blues team. His end of first year exam results were so impressive that he received a Vice-Chancellor's Award and, thereby, made his opening pitch for a Starred First, come the end of his undergraduate course. He joined the Union and became a popular speaker. That old surprise of Chinese features producing unadulterated Queen's English still captivated his first-time audience and retained the support of those who came to know him of old.

Whilst acknowledged as a rare talent, he was not unique. Anita del Azura at least emulated him, possibly even out-pointed him in one particular respect. She was Cuban. At Cambridge, there were students from all over the world, thus Jeremy was but one amongst many overseas' students. Least represented were the few remaining hard-line Communist nations. Cuba boasts an excellent education system of its own; its citizens are not globetrotters. It was Anita's exceptional intellectual ability that had paved her way to one of the world's most highly regarded universities. Anita was the Carmen of academia: raven haired, smouldering eyed, petite, lissom, and explosive. Proud (some would say arrogant), intolerant of the mediocre, and untainted by the hypocrisy of false modesty, she was at Cambridge to challenge, not to kowtow. Nature had provided her with a scimitar-sharp mind; here, she proposed to temper and to hone it into a precision instrument. Having achieved the highest mark possible in her first degree, she had won an international scholarship for post-graduate study in Politics. To have been allowed to expose herself to the corruptive atmosphere of capitalist privilege and preference, which this ancient seat of learning represented, was indicative of the faith her state had invested in her.

That she and Jeremy should gravitate towards one another, despite their totally contrary cultural origins, had about it a degree of inevitability. Separately, they overshadowed all others; together, they blazed. It was her volcanic mind and temperament, as much as her Latin looks, that fascinated and mesmerised Jeremy. So utterly different from what he had encountered either at home or during his time in England, thus far. He, so biddable and anxious to avoid causing offence; she, who could not give a damn what destruction she left in her wake: a rare coupling.

Rare and frequently unstable. Cream teas were soured. Punting parties foundered. Long and lazy summer evening discussions in pub courtyards ended abruptly. Doors were slammed and objects were thrown; ideology vied with principle; certainty with newly-realised insecurity. Common sense dictated that this relationship offered Jeremy nothing but pain, confusion, and distraction. Home had imbued him with obedience; school had equipped him with the confidence that can flourish within carefully controlled boundaries; his first two years at university had confirmed his innate capacity to glitter and to dazzle on home territory: academia, football, formal debating, casual and uncomplicated friendships. Anita, blown into his life by a hurricane of her own creating, uprooted everything about life that Jeremy had previously mastered.

Suddenly, the once assured Starred-First was in jeopardy. Jeremy's Tutor asked him to drop-in for sherry - a Cambridge code: Tutorial sherry = concern and counselling. Dr. E. G. L. Manderville combined the intellectual logic of a Chemical Engineer with the innocence of a man who had been born but a few streets distance from the College rooms he now occupied; they, themselves, were just a corridor away from where he had lived, both as an undergraduate and research student. Universally known as "Dr. Manderville", not even the internet could reveal for what names E.G.L. stood.

"Ah, Chan, do come in, do come in. Select your seat, sir; cast books, papers, or cat aside. Fino, Manzanilla, or Old Oloroso? May I recommend the Oloroso, should you be no especial aficionado?" Dr. Manderville was as old-school as Fothergill, remembered by Jeremy from his father's tales, but kindlier. He was an academic of considerable renown, much published, and feted by industrialists, who had benefited from his meticulous work. He lived his life curiously positioned between the cutting-edge of his laboratory and the timelessness of his College Rooms; between the now and the never; between reality and romance. "Good of you to drop-by, sir, good of you." The gas fire hissed. Like the sherry and the elderly don, it emanated a comforting warmth. It ameliorated the stark silence that followed.

"Was there something particular, Dr. Manderville?" Jeremy posited.

"Particular? Ah yes, particular. Erm, what think you of the Oloroso? An unfairly (and unwisely) neglected pleasure, in my opinion. An old fashioned wine, of course. Not suited to the cocktail lounge. Not for 'mixologists', as I believe they call themselves, but worthy of note, nevertheless. In my opinion. Yes. Yes, indeed."

"The sherry's most welcome. Thank you."

"My pleasure, sir. My pleasure. Will you take another glass? Yes, another glass is called for, I surmise."

"Thank you. Your good health, Dr. Manderville. But, returning to the particular reason for your kind invitation?"

"Yes, indeed. Yes. Erm, the term. How goes the term, sir?"

"Fine. Good, thanks. A little behind with my work but, you know.... ."

"Ah, work. Now that's the thing. Work. Yes. Work."

"Are you dissatisfied with my performance, Dr. Manderville?"

"A direct mind, sir. Not a quality of my own but a quality, indeed. 'Dissatisfied': an inadequate word, in my opinion. It augurs discontent but fails to specify its causes. My lexicographical colleagues may wonder at its usage. To be satisfied, now: that is clear. To be sated, to be full, an entirety. 'Dis' would imply the opposite but is to be dissatisfied to be empty? Not in its current deployment. But, then, to be how lacking, if not wholly empty? An unsatisfactory word. In my opinion."

Dr. Manderville seemed more at ease during his disquisition. Its ending left him, once again, lost for words. Once more, the hissing gas fire filled the conversational void. Then, quite suddenly, "A Starred-First, now. A rare accomplishment. Rare, indeed. In my opinion. Yours for the asking, sir. Once."

"Are you beginning to doubt my ability to achieve it?" Jeremy asked, not defiantly, nor even challengingly. He asked the question forensically.

"Ability! Now there's a word I like. Ability may be measured. Two years of study and examination have established your ability, sir. In my opinion. No, I doubt not your ability. And ability, now; no Starred-First was ever achieved without ability. But application, too, sir. Application is essential. In my opinion. Essential, er, yes; essential."

"And, *in your opinion*," (just a hint of satirical emphasis in Jeremy's voice, here,) "my application has been lacking of late?"

"Direct, again, sir! Most direct. Er, 'lacking', now: another unsatisfactory word, as it is used in modern parlance. Another 'nothing' word which does not fit the circumstance..."

Jeremy interrupted. "But you think I have lost clarity of focus?"

"Ah, focus! Yes. A most helpful interjection. I thank you, sir. Clarity of focus: quintessential to the securing of a Starred-First. A drop more Oloroso?"

Dr. Manderville sensed that his concern had been conveyed. He was mightily relieved that it had been managed without reference to Anita del Azura. She occupied the passion and the cunning of Politics; his was the logical and practical world of Chemical

Engineering. The only likely outcome of combining the two disciplines was pyrotechnic - in his opinion.

Surprises All-Round.

Potent though the allure of Anita was, Jeremy's curious exchange with Dr. Manderville made its mark. His fascination remained but he broke his captive bonds, renewed his depleted application and ended his final year with the rare accolade of a Starred-First. Gerald and Geraldine were delighted, as, indeed, was Dr. Manderville. Post-Graduate research was the obvious next project to embark upon.

But Anita's was a two year scholarship and the fascination she afforded Jeremy, now free from his focus upon Finals, remained.

The pattern of Gerald and Geraldine's annual travels had acquired the regularity of an almanac. Chinese New Year was celebrated in America, where relatives lived. Visits to England occurred every eighteen months. Fortunately, the Cambridge Degree Ceremonies had coincided with one of these fixed-time visits: July. The next visit was not due until a year the following January. By this time, Anita would be returned to Cuba and Jeremy would be over a year into his Doctoral researches. There appeared to be no impediment to her to moving into the ample flat that Jeremy had been able to secure with the "red bag" money his academic achievement had earned him.

Doors continued to be slammed. Objects were still thrown. Their counter-cultural collisions remained part of their everyday existence. The pyrotechnical display had not diminished. But they both thrived: she was not willing to allow their personal chemistry to diminish her academic achievement, so important to the state which was paying for it; he had managed to devise a flat/lab. life-style division that ensured no further exchanges over sherry with Dr. Manderville or his PhD supervisor were deemed to be necessary. It was a most agreeable arrangement.

Gerald had insisted upon a key to the Cambridge flat for himself. Jeremy had made nothing of this, at the time. His acquired Westernisation was not so pronounced that he considered his father's Oriental "parent privilege" worthy of challenge. Given the eighteen month interlude between visits to the UK, it was a non-issue. Anita had disagreed. For her, it was a point of principle. An individual's personal liberty was as precious as that of a whole society. Paternalism, patronage, patriarchs were discredited history and had no place in the modern age. Jeremy should make a stand against his father's mediaevalism just as assuredly as the world's peasants should oppose the landowners, slaves their masters, women male domination. It was a matter of duty. Although he had lived in the West for nearly a decade, now, Jeremy's concept of duty, formed from the cradle, differed from Anita's. Hers was political ideology, his was familial. Both were cultural expectations. Yet another tempestuous impasse ensued; yet another reconciliation followed.

Gerald and Geraldine arrived at Cambridge Station about mid-morning. Jeremy was in his lab.; Anita was reading an essay to her tutor. The visit had not been pre-announced.

A short taxi drive brought Jeremy's parents to the flat that their generous gift had allowed him to purchase. They paid the driver, entered the communal vestibule, took the lift to the first floor, and used their key to enter. It would be, they thought, a most pleasant surprise for their son, when he returned from his research lab.

Although he had known Anita for well over a year, he had never mentioned her in his letters home. It was not that he felt any shame in his relationship with her but neither did he feel mention of it would be received with acclamation. It was merely part of the developing complexity of his life that had begun the day he had been handed-over to Charlie Wimpole's care.

Gerald and Geraldine took their cases to the guest room and unpacked. They lay on the bed for a short nap, following their long and tiring journey. It was from this nap that they were roused by the sound of a key in the lock, followed by someone entering, laden with supermarket carrier-bags, which were taken directly to the kitchen. Cupboard and fridge doors were opened and closed, as the bags' contents were transferred. Running water could be heard, as the kettle was filled. A radio was turned on. They did not stir from the bed. Not because they were still too tired. Not because they wished to prolong their moment of surprise. They did not stir because they had seen something of the person who had entered and passed by their bedroom door, which was ajar. It had not been Jeremy. At least, they assumed it had not been Jeremy, for their fleeting glimpse had caught sight of a skirt swishing past.

Anita habitually returned home first. In academia, "essay-based" subjects tend to operate between 10.00 and 3.00; "lab.-based" subjects occupy longer hours. She was happy to shop and to cook; Jeremy dealt with the clearing-up.

Gerald and Geraldine were unsure of what to do next.

Feisty though Anita's manner was, she was far from being clumsy. She was more ballerina than bombardier. The banging and crashing in the kitchen was strategic, not habitual. From the moment she had entered the flat she had recognized an intrusive presence. It was a realisation activated, not by the partially closed Guest Room door, nor by a fleeting glimpse of bodies on the bed. She had *seen* nothing untoward. But she had sensed the presence of a stranger (or strangers.) She had *smelled* it. The scent was faint yet distinct and assertive. It was also alien to the flat she had occupied for several months. She had last been aware of it in Cuba. It was camphor, used there to impregnate candles, in order to keep irritating evening bugs at bay. Since first arriving in England, until now, she had never encountered that familiar contradiction of acrid sweetness.

Odd though the adult Gerald had long-since recognised the habits of Fothergill's to have been, one of them he had failed to slough-off: a firm belief in the necessity of moth-balls in order to keep tightly-packed clothing in good order. Impossible to buy, any longer, in the UK, KL still boasted General Stores in which they were readily available. Gerald (and, thus, Geraldine) never travelled without them. Their trade-mark pong had invaded the magnolia-scented ambience of hotel rooms, world-wide.

Captive in the kitchen, Anita *knew* her space had been invaded. Grounded in the Guest Room, Gerald and Geraldine were equally aware that someone other than their son had gained open access to the flat. Neither party felt safe to stray beyond the confines they currently occupied.

A couple of hours passed.

Anita noisily prepared supper for herself and Jeremy. Gerald and Geraldine maintained a monastic silence.

"Hi, I'm home!" Jeremy burst through the door in an exuberant mood. "How's your day been?" This interrogative became unexpectedly exaggerated by its combining a routine question with a suddenly recognised, yet wholly unanticipated, smell. He stopped and sniffed significantly.

"Come straight to the kitchen, Jeremy!" An imperious plea. "*Now!*"

This exchange did nothing to alleviate Gerald and Geraldine's anxiety. For some time, they had been sitting, back-to-back, on the two edges of the bed. It took but seconds from Jeremy's arrival for the quotient of in-flat tension to increase. Unlike the other three, he did not suffer the anxiety of unknowingness. Worse-off than they, he knew exactly what had occurred. His boarding school days had been scented by moth-balls. He knew the source of the smell, yet he could scarcely believe it.

Lean Pickings.

As a Cuban, albeit an affluent Cuban, Anita was well-versed in transforming supper for few into supper for rather more. Although no "loaves-and-fishes" turn, what she placed upon the kitchen table for her unexpected guests was appealing, both to eye and to appetite. Salad leaves glistened in their dressing and the clever incorporation of Sesame Oil lent it immediate attraction to an Oriental palate. Two fillets of chicken, now cubed and combined with that age-old Cuban standby, rice and beans, offered a focal dish that proved to be more than sufficiently substantial. Bananas, sliced and mixed with grapes, orange segments, sugar, rum, and cream ensured that the meal concluded on a note of comforting confection.

Tasty and welcome though this impromptu meal was, it failed to seduce Gerald and Geraldine into free-flowing conversation. Stiff, formal introductions gave way to awkward silence. Jeremy's polite enquiries about the flight from KL were met with clipped and truncated responses. Whilst she had risen to the occasion in the kitchen, Anita was not disposed to play the part of ameliorator. She considered her space to have been invaded. Her natural inclination was to oppose the colonisers and to assert her freedom. To play the part of Che to the Chans' Batista. Smouldering rage oozed from her pores, like sweat. Jeremy seemed to shed his skin of Cambridge confidence and to emerge cowed. The swaying, mesmerising seducer of Eve in Eden, fallen on his belly prone.

Coffee was served. Gerald and Geraldine claimed jet-lag and returned to the Guest-Room. Jeremy set about clearing. Anita sat in incandescent silence, blindly turning the pages of a magazine. Darkness fell, outside, but she made no move to draw the curtains. Nothing could be further from her current preoccupation than cosy domesticity. Cosy domesticity was what Jeremy craved but recognised he would be denied.

***

He was awake, the next morning, earlier than usual. Anita was still sleeping, so he slipped, deftly, out of bed and closed the bedroom door behind him, carefully and quietly. No trace of camphor lingered in the hallway. The Guest-Room door and window were wide open and there was no suggestion that his parents had ever occupied it. On the kitchen table was a sheet of A4 paper. It was headed: *To: Chan, Hong-Chun*. What followed was equally terse and impersonal: *Expect developed correspondence, forthwith*. There was no form of signing-off.

Whilst delighted to note that she had seen-off her uninvited and unwelcome invaders, Anita was not minded to soften her manner towards Jeremy. To repel the enemy was one thing; to instil the spirit of revolution within the fibre of the people, so long suppressed and compliant, was a different matter, altogether. Resolve was required. She set-off for the library, much earlier than usual, having appeared deaf to Jeremy's nervous attempts at communication. Miserably, he travelled alone to his lab.

A Cambridge Starred First in Chemical Engineering tends not to result in post-graduate research into methods of producing large quantities of cheap fertiliser, designed to turn barren Third World countries into self-sustaining grain belts. Governments – or, rather, Intelligence Services - have other work in mind for such talent. Only Jeremy's Professor knew, precisely, the volatile work upon which his lab. was engaged. Jeremy's role, under his guidance, was to conduct a series of experiments that investigated the behaviour of various chemicals in combination with each other. Shortly after having first registered as a PhD student, he had received a letter from Professor Quentin Tinniswood, inviting him to discuss a possible programme of work. Tinniswood's reputation was restricted to a narrow field of specialists but, amongst that small group, his name was near-sacred. For him to initiate communication with so recent a graduate as Jeremy indicated a very special interest. Not to respond enthusiastically was unthinkable.

It was arranged that Jeremy would visit the Professor at his house, a few miles removed from Cambridge, and in a rather isolated location. Quentin Tinniswood eschewed the limelight of College Feasts and Media Exposure. His photograph never appeared on the back cover of his many publications, nor did he permit the habitual précis of his life and work to feature. He delivered few public lectures, had not taught undergraduates for decades, and he ran his own, somewhat solitary, lab., in which he worked substantially alone. The University Authorities had learned neither to take an interest in his work nor to interfere with it. To all intents and purposes, he did not exist beyond a tightly controlled cordon.

All correspondence, preparatory to Jeremy's visit, had been delivered by hand. No stamps, no post-office, no college pigeon hole. Seemingly chance encounters with strangers had resulted in an exchange of envelopes. *No one, absolutely no one* was to be told about the liaison. Even Anita was unaware of these measures and, subsequently, of under whose supervision Jeremy's research was being conducted.

That initial meeting had been mesmerising. A driver had been dispatched to collect and deliver Jeremy to the Professor's house, hidden away in a remote pocket of an equally remote location. The bell had been answered and the door opened by a small, anonymous-looking lady, prematurely aged in appearance but defined by piercingly bright and intelligent-looking eyes. She wore a small-print floral dress, a cardigan, and a simple gold chain around her neck. An equally simple gold band surrounded her left second finger. This was the Professor's wife, never known as Mrs. Tinniswood but by her professional name: Dr. Hermione Carstairs. She, too, was a Chemical Engineer. She had been, years ago, Quentin Tinniswood's first and, until now, only PhD student.

"Mr. Chan, how good of you to come all this way. Do enter."
An educated, "old Cambridge", voice: crisp articulation,
chiselled enunciation, precise syntax. "Would you care for
coffee - or do you agree that we are close enough to lunchtime
for gin? I *do so hope* you concur!" Her bright blue eyes
twinkled, mischievously, as her deeply-cut crows' feet framed
their resolve.

"Gin would be most welcome, thank you."

"Good man! Quentin rarely, if indeed ever, makes a
misjudgement! He and I enjoy it with tap-water but we have
mixers for guests. Why employ an army of blenders, testers, and
tasters to ensure the botanicals are in perfect equipoise, only to
wreak molecular mayhem with additives such as tonic water,
lime, even coca-cola, I'm led to believe! One may as well start
with potcheen or turnip vodka!"

"As a Chemical Engineer, I can but agree with you; as a drinker
of gin, I have always enjoyed a little tonic."

"Excellent, excellent: the young man has a mind of his own and
the courage of his convictions! As I said, Quentin never
misjudges."

The drinks were prepared. Just the two. Dr. Carstairs headed for
a small conservatory extension, full of cane furniture and potted
plants. "Do sit," she proffered, and placed Jeremy's drink close
to him on an occasional table.

It was a glorious, late-summer's day. The sun was still high
enough in the sky to offer warmth without glare; the hopper
windows were all open, as was the conservatory door, which led

into a garden somewhat larger than the facade of the house had indicated to be likely. A well-tended central lawn was surrounded by borders, themselves filled with roses, foxgloves and hollyhocks, delphiniums, aquilegia, Johnson Blue geraniums, Japanese anemones, phlox, penstemons, and lupins. An apple tree (Beauty of Bath) occupied one far corner of the lawn; a Victoria Plum tree, the other. This view was a microcosm of "calendar England".

"Quentin will join us, shortly," Jeremy's hostess noted. "Meanwhile, do tell me a little of yourself."

She was easy to talk with, exhibiting genuine interest, happy to pick-up the thread of a theme that was in danger of fraying, adept at flitting from topic to topic. She also exhibited largesse with the gin bottle. Thus, when the Professor finally made his appearance, Jeremy was mellow and at-ease.

As a top-flight academic, Jeremy was aware of Tinniswood's expertise but, given the Professor's chosen anonymity, the younger man would not have recognised the elder, not even on his home-ground, had he not been introduced. Quentin Tinniswood was a police-photo-fit-artist's nightmare. He could be aged anywhere between 40 and 65; his hair colour was neutral; he had no distinguishing facial features; he was of average height, build, weight. He did not wear glasses; he dressed conventionally, and no hint of the region of his birth and upbringing may be detected in his impeccable R.P. delivery. His name aside, he lacked any sense of individuality.

"Glad you were able to visit, Mr. Chan. No need to ask if Hermione's been looking after you; it's something she does extraordinarily well. Thank you, m'dear." This, both in general gratitude and for the glass of gin spirited out of the air with the deftness of a magician producing silk handkerchiefs. "Your very good health - and here's to *success*." This final element of the toast seemed to be laden with significance.

Hermione retired to the kitchen. Jeremy awaited the Professor's lead. The Professor savoured his gin and replenished it.

Suddenly: "You have an interesting background, Mr. Chan." For a while it looked as if this may be a *non sequitor*. Then, eventually, "The Chinese, in what we now call Malaysia, have done very well for themselves. May I posit a question: is their loyalty pan-Sino or Malaysia-specific? No need to answer. Not yet. You have pretty deep anglophile roots. Indeed, whilst you have the physical features of your race, you have the voice and manner of a well-educated Brit. Another question to ponder: in these matters, *what precisely* do you *feel* yourself to be? Let me crystallize: would you consider yourself to be Western or Oriental; Chinese, Malaysian, or British; any of the above or a Citizen of the World? But we must not allow Hermione's efforts in the kitchen to spoil. Bring your drink with you. Shall I lead the way?"

That initial meeting had led, rapidly, to further exchanges and, ultimately, to Jeremy becoming a research student under the Professor's supervision.

That had been August. In September, Anita had moved into the flat. Gerald and Geraldine had paid their unexpected visit in mid-November. Today, Jeremy needed to wrestle with issues quite equal in complexity to those thrown-up by Chemical

Engineering.   And there was something echoing in his mind. Something Professor Tinniswood had emphasised before any documents of agreement had been signed and finalised: "In our work, Mr. Chan, personal relationships do not exist.   No pillow-talk; no debate; no intrusion.   Our work is everything; all else is nothing."

***

"Hi, I'm home.   How was your day?"

Just as *his* day had begun with a sheet of A4, so did it end.

Jeremy,

I shall not leave, voluntarily; you will need to expel me.   I shall be away, visiting friends, for a few days.   You have decisions to reach and to make.   A.

Epistolary.

Contrary to the practice he had adopted from Jeremy's first going away to school, Gerald's letter was written in Mandarin. In its formality of style and expression, it might have been either a state treaty or a business contract. Any personal hurt, anger, regret, or disappointment that may have informed it was not made apparent.

In effect, Gerald regarded the Red Bag money that Jeremy had used to purchase the Cambridge flat to be "money-in-trust". It was his intention to break that trust and, thus, to take steps to put the flat on the market, forthwith. Further, Jeremy was to withdraw from his PhD programme, settle any outstanding debts, and catch the earliest possible flight back to KL. A position within the Company would be secured for him; he would live in the family home until such time that his earnings and savings made it possible for him to purchase his own property. No more needed to be said.

To reply in Mandarin or in English? A complex question that required all of Jeremy's intellectual agility to resolve. What effect was he seeking to make? Was he at war with his father or in negotiation? Did he wish to heal or to amputate? Was his intention to face-down his opposition or to side-step it?

He decided upon English.

Dear Mother & Father,

That I should find myself writing this letter, at all, shocks and saddens me as much as its contents will shock and sadden you. This correspondence is NOT of my making.

That your intended pleasant surprise visit should have resulted in such pain is ever to be regretted. That you should have reacted as you have is cause for even greater regret.

In an ideal world, you would have been aware that Anita shared the flat with me, without needing to have stumbled upon the fact. We do not live in an ideal world. Why had I not told you? Because you would have taken the steps you plan now to take, immediately. Why would you have done this? Not because you are prudes. Not because you hold high principles in regard of sexual morality. But because she is Cuban. Or, rather, because she is not Chinese.

You sent me to the West to be 'educated' but educated is not what you intended me to be. Schooled, trained, qualified, yes, but not educated. To explain the derivation of the word to you may seem pompous but it is necessary. "Education", as a linguistic concept, demands that the recipient is led OUT of his/her habitual narrowness. Expansion of mind, outlook, prospects: this was never part of your plan. You, father, suffered Fothergill's because it was an unavoidable part of the whole you sought: knowledge and qualifications to return home and advance the fortunes of the family firm. A facility with English aside, you are no less KL Chinese than ever you were as a boy. Nor do you expect me to be. But you are wrong. Wrong in your expectation; wrong in your misunderstanding of my assimilation.

Whilst your generous gift enabled me to buy the flat, it was I who bought it; not you; it is registered under my signature. Legally, no matter what strings you attempt to pull and no matter how resolved you may be, you cannot sell it. But I can and I shall, for I need to relocate.

As to my returning to KL: NO, NO, NO! My research is nothing to do with personal vanity. It is of importance. Quintessential importance. I cannot and I will not abandon it.

With sad regrets for unavoidable hurt caused.

Your loving but compromised son,

Jeremy.

Chemical Reaction.

The notes left by Anita +Gerald (and Geraldine), combined with his parents' ensuing letter, triggered responses that none of them had anticipated. Pliant Jeremy had been rendered tensile. Anything-to-avoid-a-rift-Jeremy had become Jeremy-will-forge-his-own-destiny-regardless-of-the-cost. Anita could stay or she could leave; she could simper or she could sulk, it was a matter of indifference to him. His parents could accept the stance he had adopted or they could disown him. That was their choice; their responsibility. The young man who had relied upon a pleasant manner to ensure a comfortable popularity no longer gave a damn; his natural courtesy had crystallised into abrasiveness; a mild manner was transmogrified into menace. To all intents and purposes so different from each other, his parents and his mistress had fused into a paradoxical catalyst – each party had set-out to claim him for themselves, neither had emerged from the process in possession but both had contributed to his transformation. They may be the same as ever they had been; Jeremy was now different. Irredeemably different. That was his express intention.

The pampered daughter of indulgent parents and an admiring extended family, Anita's life experience had equipped her with no devices to counter Jeremy's obdurate opposition. A toss of her raven-black hair, a stamp of her elegant foot, petulance, political slogans, and *parti-pris* had been her habitual armoury. In this particular campaign she found herself to be wrongly munitioned and, thus, incapable of making an advance. Mr. & Mrs. Chan fared no better. A tradition of respect for elders and the instructional role of parents, had been their life-long stand-by. What had proven itself to be a powerful strategy against a compliant child was rendered toothless in the face of adamantine resolve.

Jeremy put the flat into the hands of an estate agent, whom he instructed to seek-out an alternative property. He packed his bags and moved into temporary B & B accommodation. He advised the agent of Anita's presence in the flat, explaining that he was unsure of her intentions but authorising him to ask her to move out, should she linger, and once he had secured a buyer. He paid for a Post Office forwarding address but decided against issuing changed details to anyone other than the estate agent and Professor Tinniswood, both of whom he instructed to regard the information as restricted.

However, it was never his intention to hide, nor to be reclusive. He wandered around Cambridge openly and without feeling the need to glance over his shoulder. He had no qualms about bumping into Anita; indeed, he welcomed the prospect but he harboured no scheme to engineer it. Like the materials he mixed and exposed to temperature changes in his lab., he had become a product. "We are all products," he reasoned, "all subjected to combination and to manipulation. None of us is stable, within the chemical definition. Mutability is our natural state. Rock becomes gemstone; liquid becomes gas; fusion and fission are as close as is their spelling - and as far apart."

With this at the forefront of his mind, he settled into his new pattern of life. The estate agent made no mention of Anita but did report that he had secured a buyer. A few weeks later, he wrote to say that Jeremy may care to view a new flat which he felt would be ideal. Jeremy sold, bought, and re-settled. He set-off for his lab. ever-earlier and returned from it ever-later. This was not escapism; it was involvement. The area of research that Professor Tinniswood had outlined at their first meeting proved to be of fascination to Jeremy's enquiring mind. Multiple complexities and perplexities exuded. They made the subject even more fascinating. They were to the academic Chemist what cryptic clues are to the crossword solver. Whilst the first weeks had indicated the possibilities for research, those which followed began to suggest the practical application an Engineer might lend those possibilities, for the greater good of humankind.

Curiosity was giving way to compulsion.

A Secret Profession.

As a young man, Quentin Tinniswood had feared that his physical ordinariness would shunt him into a life of marginalised anonymity. Perhaps it was this fear that had spurred him to efforts of heroic proportion in his bid to master the detail of Chemical Engineering so absolutely that he was awarded a Professorship at an unusually early stage in his Cambridge career. That event and the unexpected approach that almost immediately followed it was his first and last experience of celebrity status.

A brilliant academic career as an undergraduate and research student had led him, naturally, into university teaching which, itself, required him to undertake continuous advanced research. For a few years his career pattern had followed that of the many who had come before him. He lectured and examined; he worked in his lab.; he sought solutions to problems that hindered technological and industrial advancement. In this latter role, he acquired a reputation for thoroughness and practicality. Little he did was radical; rather, he was prepared, painstakingly, to correct the minutiae of previous efforts that had foundered, in order to discover the fine-tuning required to transform failure into function.

Then, suddenly, he received the unexpected, unapplied for, invitation to head his own department. He was not to replace anyone; no existing departmental organisation was to change; his was to be a new venture. He must understand that such beginnings were to be small in scale, at first. A previously dilapidated and somewhat obscurely sited building was to be converted into additional lab. space. "And Faculty Politics need to be avoided at all costs, here, Tinniswood. The green-eyed god stalks the corridors of Chemical Engineering just as surely as it visits those of Social Science and the Liberal Arts. Our innate practicality, alas, does not foreswear Man's baser nature." The speaker was the Deputy Vice-Chancellor of the University and it was he who had made Dr. Tinniswood the offer of a Professorship. The burden of his caution was that the newly-furbished lab. should be occupied quietly (if not silently) and that work within it should begin without announcement nor advertisement.

Quentin was starting to realise that it was his natural anonymity, which, once, he had feared may exclude him, to which, now, he owed his advancement. His departure from his previous place of work would not receive much attention. When there, he had worked alone, rather than as a team member, re-calibrating his predecessors' near-misses. Work too dull for his colleagues to take much, if any, interest in. His meticulously prepared, but rather pedantic and sparsely-attended lectures would not be missed. He had not, thus far, been asked to supervise any research students who would need to be transferred. This was to be an arrangement as covert as an undercover exercise but without the attendant intrigue.

The Office of Deputy Vice-Chancellor was, itself, an innovation. Its current holder was the first in post. Traditionalists amongst the Fellows had decried the appointment. The University had managed for centuries without such an Officer, why should one need to be created? What was to be the function of such? Would this creation detract from and, thus, diminish the role of Vice-Chancellor? If so, to what purpose; worse still, to what effect? Few of these questions had been treated with sufficient regard to provide acceptable answers. Interestingly, and unusually, there had been no equal and opposite pioneering voice to counter that of the traditionalists. No one, other than the Deputy Vice-Chancellor, himself, seemed to consider establishment of the Office to be either necessary or desirable.

Just as his position was judged to be either suspicious or irrelevant, so too was its holder. Sir Edward Fitzmaurice was not an academic. Once, years ago, he had taken a Bachelor's degree (which he had subsequently converted into a Master's via a cheque in an envelope) but those three years had been his only previous close experience of university life. He had made a small fortune in Industry and then diverted his attention to Politics. As a member of the party-in-government, he held a junior ministerial brief.

"So glad you understand the potential delicacy of this, Tinniswood. All nonsense, of course, but nonsense can be such an embuggeration to worthwhile progress. So, in short: you accept the professorship; you are untroubled that there will be no enthronement ceremony; the lab. space on offer is restricted but refurbished; at present, you will be working single-handed but research students may be directed to you in due course of time. Is there anything else?"

"Just one detail. Am I correct in thinking that you wish me to continue with the sort of work I have been doing?"

"Mr. Fix-It - my apologies - *Professor* Fix-It, aren't you?"

"In a manner of speaking, yes."

"Just the ticket! Of course, there will be some fine-tuning but, in essence, yes, you will carry on with your current line of work." Having a mind given to the examination of minutiae, Quentin's resonated in response to certain ill-defined phrases: "fine-tuning", "in essence", "line of".

"May I ask you to be a little more specific?"

"Today's meeting is to establish a broad picture. Details will follow - all in good time. You can rely upon me," blustered the Deputy Vice-Chancellor. A man used to creating the rules of the game, rather than playing to them. "You can rely upon me" was another resonant phrase that failed to quell Quentin's growing apprehension.

"Perhaps it is I who should be a little more specific," Quentin responded. "Who will select the projects upon which I will be working?"

"Is that significant? I thought it was *the work* you relished; the intellectual challenge; the triumph of succeeding where others have failed. *That's* what I'm offering you!" This last comment, simple though its language may have been, was expressed in a complex tone: amusement; frustration; dismissal; the threat to take back what had already been given. Each of these co-existed and in equal measure. "Anyway, I have to rush. Bloody meetings! Rarely get a moment to myself. Glad to have you on board, Tinniswood. I'll be in touch."

Quentin's interview was over. The Deputy Vice-Chancellor had hooked his fish and reeled him in.

That had been many years ago. As Hermione had observed to Jeremy, over gin, "Quentin is rarely, if ever, wrong." Certainly, he had not been wrong to ask his question, "Who will select the projects upon which I will be working?" But he had not been given a straight answer.

Hermione Carstairs.

"Ah, Tinniswood!" The Deputy Vice-Chancellor's habitual clipped abruptness heralded, rather than greeted, Quentin, as he was guided into Sir Edward's office by his p.a. "Well settled, by now, I trust?" Although intended to be a question, the enunciation had turned it into a dictat. "Pull up a pew." Like a policeman's on point-duty, his hands signalled the manoeuvre Quentin was expected to execute. In the bay window space was an occasional table, much smaller than the imposing desk, near to which stood several chairs. In one of them sat a young girl; Fitzmaurice marched towards another, as if bent upon besieging it, and a third was guided by Quentin towards the table, upon which lay a manila folder. "Miss Carstairs, Professor Tinniswood; Tinniswood, Miss Hermione Carstairs. Let's sit." With wry amusement, Quentin wondered how much effort it had taken the Deputy Vice-Chancellor to insert "Let's" into the latter phrase.

Hermione Carstairs had recently graduated (brilliantly) yet her face suggested greater age and maturity than her twenty-one years. It was not an unattractive face. Eyes as blue and clear as sea-water shot through by powerful sunshine lent them an attenuated iridescence. Her skin had seen a great deal more soap-and-water than make-up, which lent it an aura of wholesomeness. It was a face that belonged much more to a scholar than to a party-girl and it radiated a sense of purpose.

"Right, to business!" Sir Edward, although totally unaware of Quentin's musings, scattered them, rather in the manner of Joshua's trumpets at Jericho. "Now, Tinniswood, this rather exceptionally gifted young lady is in need of a PhD supervisor. You are in need of a research assistant. Instant solution times two!" It was this businesslike brusqueness that Fitzmaurice felt the University lacked. "Far too much time taken up with discussion and deliberation - and both cost money, let me tell you!" was the mantra he had devised for himself. "That's her file, there," tapping the manila folder with his fleshy forefinger and talking about Hermione as if she had already left the room. "Take it, read it, and return it within 24 hours. Purely a formality, Miss Carstairs," he added, recalling her presence. "As far as I can see, lab. space can be made ready, immediately, with a view to the liaison commencing on Monday, at 9.00 a.m. sharp."

"Liaison" was one of those terms used by Sir Edward that prompted Quentin to question his meaning. Manifestly, he had no romantic development in mind, yet there was something that smacked of secrecy in the word; something covert. He was also puzzled that this meeting should have been called at all. The allocation of post-graduate students to a personal supervisor was an academic issue, not a bureaucratic one. Normally, the Senior Professor within the Faculty would assume the task. It was, thought Quentin, as if he, his small lab. space, now Hermione, were viewed by the Deputy Vice-Chancellor as a person fiefdom. One over which he exercised a political form of *droit de seignure.*

"Nothing I've overlooked?" Again, a question presented as a statement, indicating that the meeting was over.

"No, nothing I can think of," replied Quentin. "A pleasure to meet you, Miss Carstairs. Oh, and my congratulations upon your dazzling success, so far."

"A pleasure to meet you, also, Professor Tinniswood and thank you. The future is a most exciting prospect." He suddenly realised that this was the first time she had spoken. The clarity of her voice and delivery emulated that of her eyes. Like her face, there was something beyond youthfulness about her speech. But the Deputy Vice-Chancellor was on his feet and moving from the backwater of the bay window towards his desk. He had work to do and no time to waste on pleasantries. The p.a. appeared, as if summoned by some form of divinity, and the two visitors were escorted out.

***

Upon returning to his lab., Quentin settled himself and opened the manila folder, in which he found the essential details of Hermione Carstairs' life, thus far. As he read through the contents, he realised that he had been presented with much more than a C.V. To use a Fitzmaurice term, he was reading a dossier.

Hermione was the only child of Cambridge parents. Her father was employed by the Victor Gollancz publishing house and he had volunteered for service in The International Brigades, not knowing that she had been conceived shortly before his departure for Spain. He never returned; not even in a coffin. Her mother had never re-married, nor had she returned to her career as a journalist, following Hermione's birth. Both parents had come from affluent families, thus there had been sufficient money to maintain a comfortable town house, walls lined with books, rooms filled by a constant stream of visitors, all of whom were strangers to silence. There had been something faintly unreal about Hermione's childhood; something almost Edwardian in its opulence and its timeless sensuality. She read, and she talked, she sang, and she danced, and she mixed with people far older than herself. But she never played. Not with dolls; not by herself; not with other children.

At school, she was academically brilliant and socially successful. Other children liked her and she liked them. She would invite them to her house and they would reciprocate. But never to play. These were invitations to tea and to talk. She loved to talk and to listen to the talk of others. It had been, since the day of her birth, an additional form of oxygen.

Her mother had always been open with her about the father she had never met. About his political allegiances; about his idealism; about his belief in our duty to make the world a better place. In a curious way, he became her most abiding influence. When her education reached that point at which serious subject choices needed to be made, she harboured no doubts. Surrounded by books, and ideas, and discussions every day of her life, this offspring of radical publishing and journalism failed to play true-to-form: she selected Science A Levels. Thence to a Cambridge degree in Chemical Engineering and to the office of The Deputy Vice-Chancellor, in order to be allocated a PhD supervisor.

As he read through this, Quentin began to understand Hermione's face and voice. The face and the voice of a girl who had only ever been little in the physical sense; young in the sense of years spent alive.

Serious, brilliant, and successful as an undergraduate though she had been, the dossier demonstrated that Hermione was no archetypal bluestocking, however. There was to her brief existence, thus far, a political (perhaps Political might be better) agenda. Not just a father who had worked for a self-consciously Left Wing organization and who had forfeited his life to political principle; nor merely a mother whose by-line was once to be noted in the pages of *The Manchester Guardian*. Hermione's undergraduate years had been as politically active as late Fifties' propriety permitted. Restricted to internal College protests against outdated visiting rights and to outspoken speeches from the floor at Union debates, had she been but a few years younger she would, doubtless, have taken her place on the Aldermaston March.

Evidently, Sir Edward Fitzmaurice knew all about Hermione's non-academic record. He would have read the manila folder long before he had summoned her to his office in order to propose that she should become Quentin's research assistant and he her PhD supervisor. Why, he wondered, had Fitzmaurice not had the information edited, so that it reflected Hermione's academic credentials, only? Of what possible interest might the great man consider political commitment to be to someone whose own political colours were as neutral as his physical appearance? So unaffiliated was Quentin that he only ever voted if he happened to be passing the polling station and noticed there to be no queue. That Sir Edward *was* playing some game of intrigue could not be doubted but *what* game? And *why*?

***

The Manila folder had been returned, as demanded, within twenty-four hours. Quentin had attached a simple note: *Read & noted. Miss Carstairs should report to my lab. at 9.00 a.m. on Monday. Q.T.*

All this had taken place years before. Hermione Carstairs successfully completed her PhD under Professor Tinniswood's supervision. In celebration, they married. It had been an unspectacular occasion in the Cambridge Registry Office. He had worn a mid-brown herringbone sports' jacket and cavalry twill trousers; she, a small floral print dress and pale blue cardigan. Her mother and Fitzmaurice had been witnesses. There had been no other guests. A short celebratory tea had been held in Sir Edward's office, the occasional table and chairs in the bay window providing quite sufficient space. Where (or whether) they honeymooned is not recorded.

***

Quentin's lab. space had remained small for all these many years. Hermione had worked alongside him long after her Doctorate was awarded. He had published, from time to time, in a deliberately un-fanfared fashion. This had been more at the insistence of his masters than of his own volition. It was not, after all, his *real* work.

No further research graduates had been directed towards him as the years had rolled by. None, that is, until he received notice to supervise a brilliant young Chinese Malay student: one Jeremy Chan, recently awarded a Starred First.

So, Tell Me.

When Jeremy had first started to work under Professor Tinniswood's supervision, his relationship with Anita was amongst the more celebrated within the university scene. True, Dr. Manderville's Tutorial concern had tempered their conflagration but he had only damped-it-down, not extinguished it. It may have burned less brightly but with ever-increasing heat.

One of their star turns was at meetings of the Union. Pairing-up as speakers had long-since been abandoned. The result of the debates had become far too predictable. Much more spectacular was to see them adopting opposing sides of the motion, each determined to leave the other worsted. Jeremy's debating style was that of the chess-player. He liked to lay unforeseen traps for his opponent to fall for until retreat became impossible and either an increasingly discomfiting end-game was pursued or an admission of defeat was secured. Those who did not know his approach would, at first, consider him too mild mannered to be an effective debater. Others, who were long-standing initiates, relished the way in which he seemed, helplessly, to sacrifice pawns and to be almost desperately moving his more powerful pieces all over the board in a frantic bid to save them from capture. All of this was designed to mesmerise his opponent; to finesse that opponent into ill-considered bravado. Bravado soon to be transformed into ignominy. Anita's strategy was quite different. Not for her a form of Mathematics. Hers was a Latin temperament; dance rhythms pulsed in her blood-stream. The haughty stomp and the seductive backward lean of flamenco and tango informed her approach. She aimed both to terrorise and to tempt her opponents. To secure surrender or submission was her only intent; she was not interested in tactical withdrawal.

Although Professor Tinniswood paid little attention to the social scene or even to Union proceedings, he had been made aware of his new student's reputation and of his relationship with Anita. Such flamboyance flew in the face of his dictum that work was all and that personal relationships did not exist. This would explain why he had emphasised the point at their first meeting.

None the less, as Jeremy had eased his way into his new working environment, he and the professor had allowed themselves to stray into chatter that was not strictly relevant to their research.

"So, tell me," Quentin had opened, one day, "your friend, ... Anita, is it? You say she comes from Cuba?"

"That's right."

"An unusual move. Has she emigrated?"

"Oh no, she's on a Government Scholarship. A two-year Masters in Politics."

"I had no idea that the Cuban Government sponsored its students to expose themselves to the corruptive forces of the bloated Western World's discredited imperialism," chuckled the professor.

"I believe hers is an unusual case. She comes from quite an influential family. Perhaps she's been sent as a spy!"

"An interesting possibility. Anyway, enough idle chatter. How are you progressing?"

As he travelled home, that evening, Jeremy reflected on this brief exchange. On the one hand, it was little more than idle over-coffee-chatter; on the other, it was wholly contrary to the professor's clearly-stated rules of engagement. Rules that he had broken, rather than allowing himself to be wrong-footed into breaking. Of course, if he did intend to permit a more sociable strand to be introduced into the tapestry of their everyday routine, an enquiry about his girlfriend was an obvious opening gambit. Or had it, *indeed*, been a gambit? Was Tinniswood a chess-player, too? The personal interest had led very rapidly to a political one. But, if there had been any ulterior motive, this would have been an especially clumsy move, wouldn't it? Either that, or a designedly clumsy move - such as he had executed, himself, so successfully, so often. He even questioned his own role in the snatch of conversation. Had he so quickly revealed Anita's status, subject speciality, and family connections naively or was he being subconsciously disingenuous and preparing potential traps by second nature? That jest about her possibly being a spy: he was not aware of ever having posited such a suggestion before. Why should he have done so, today?

These thoughts brought him to his front door. As he opened it, he could smell something delicious drifting down the corridor from the kitchen. The prospect of supper dispersed his questions. His flat. His relationship. His research. His life. All were *so* enjoyable. He was as happy and content as he imagined it was possible to be.

It was not long after this that Gerald and Geraldine had paid their surprise visit and all had changed.

It had changed, in fact, more than he realized and it had been changing for some time. That his curiosity had been giving way to compulsion had not captured his attention – but Hermione Carstairs, who still worked alongside her husband, had noticed it. Noticed and noted.

Disorientation.

When they read his reply to their letter, Jeremy's parents were staggered. Not for one moment had it occurred to either of them that their son would do anything other than to accept and obey their instructions. Nothing within their lives' experience had equipped them for his rebellion. It was outside the pale of their cultural definition. It did not even offer them anything to discuss; it was beyond their comprehension just as much as the Astro-Physics of Stephen Hawking would be, were they called upon to debate it. Only one speculation made any sense to them: their son had gone mad.

For days they co-existed in a vacuum of silence. After a week, and for the first time in his life, Gerald recognised that he was out of control. Not at school in KL, not at Fothergill's, not at university, not at work had he ever taken a day off, before. He could not make the call, himself. Geraldine had to phone his office to say that he was unwell and unable to come-in. For the whole of that week neither of them either ate or slept properly. The maid tried to tempt them with their favourite dishes but appetite had deserted them. They would push the food around their plates, purposelessly, and eventually place the tiniest morsel on their tongues. But their throats immediately contracted; even a few grains of rice became impossible to swallow. They would sit in separate rooms, breathing deeply, in an attempt to calm racing hearts, eye-lids closed against a world they found too painful to acknowledge. Hours would pass and they would not move. They were awaiting the gathering darkness, when the blinds could be drawn and they could retreat even further from life. They went to bed ridiculously early and often fell asleep immediately, only to awaken half-an-hour later and then to lie for hours, and hours, and hours. Only sheer physical and emotional exhaustion prompted slumber in the wee-small-hours. But it did not last for long. Then came the sweats: oozing from their brows, flowing down their chests, forming little lakes in any dimple that could be located. Soaking the bed linen, as if they had been incontinent. A sauna for seconds, thereafter a de-frosting freezer.

"What have we done?" Geraldine eventually summoned-up sufficient courage to ask.

"Our duty, as parents," riposted Gerald. These eight words constituted the nearest to a conversation an entire week availed.

After ten days of this torture, the germ of a plan began to develop in Geraldine's mind. Its formation increased her frustration for she knew that it could not be executed, once finalised, whilst Gerald was in the house. His pride would not permit it.

Fourteen days after receiving Jeremy's letter, Gerald reluctantly answered the telephone. It was his p.a. She hoped he was feeling a little better; she was so sorry to disturb him but she didn't know what else to do; a problem had arisen in the factory; a problem that required Gerald's personal attention; was there the remotest possibility that she could send a car to collect him? Did she not consider it to be of the utmost importance she wouldn't have called.

Gerald's p.a. was a consummate professional. As would be true of anyone in her position, she had witnessed industrial crises before; she had sufficient experience to know when to batten-down the hatches and ride-out the storm - when to press the panic button. Gerald knew this and knew her loyalty. Were he to ignore this plea for his presence, he might be adding further loss to that of a son. If he could avert such a tragedy, he owed it to the honoured memory of his father to act. "Send the car," he assented.

Geraldine had no idea how much time she had. Although her husband had not articulated to her his thoughts in response to the 'phone call, "to act" was her reciprocal intention. The moment the sound of the engine faded, she found writing paper, pen and an envelope.

Dear Mr. Charlie,

I hardly know how to start this letter and I may have very little time to write and post it. Please forgive any errors in style or approach. ....

Whether or not Charlie Wimpole was still on the staff of Jeremy's old school Geraldine had not the first notion. Nearly four years had passed since her son had started at Cambridge. But who else could she turn to? She knew that it was pointless approaching any of her Chinese friends. To her knowledge, none had any relevant experience to draw upon and, even if they had, 'saving face' would dictate that they could never admit to it. Charlie was her only hope.

It would not be appropriate for you to write a reply to this letter in the usual manner. Gerald would recognize the envelope. May I ask you to fax a response on any evening between 6.00 and 6.30 p.m. (KL time)? I love and respect my husband but, also, I know him. This way, he will remain unaware.

As she signed the letter, she felt as if she were sending a *billet doux* to a lover. Or, rather, she felt all of the guilt and none of the excitement.

***

Charlie Wimpole received Geraldine's letter, read it, re-read it, placed it on his desktop, and groaned aloud.

"Oh bloody hell! *Yes!*" A knock at the door had followed immediately upon his recognition that Geraldine's letter had presented him with a problem of Gordian Knot proportions.

***

That he had received no response, given that his parents must have received what he had written over a fortnight ago, generated contradictory emotions within Jeremy. Part of him was relieved: it meant that he did not have yet another difficult letter to compose; another part of him was frustrated: had it been delivered? Were mislaid letters merely plot devices in Literature or might they actually exist? Yet another part of him verged upon the sulky child: had they received the letter and adjudged it to be a post-teen rant that was best ignored? Even worse, had they decided that their parental responsibility had come to an end and left him to his own devices? In short: did they no longer love him?

And what of Anita? She seemed untroubled about seeking him out. Had she deserted him, too? As Oscar Wilde might have quipped: 'to lose two people whom one loves is a misfortune; to lose three smacks of carelessness.' A witty debating line at the Union; cheap and trite in actuality.

Once longer than a fortnight had become a month and the new flat had been secured, he surmised that he was alone. It was necessary to work upon creating a carapace. People may be petulant and intemperate; work offers constancy. *His* kind of work, especially. It was no longer the prospect of a Doctorate that motivated him. Of much greater worth was a Cause. This was something that elegant phraseology, crystalline delivery, and eyes, clear and cobalt, had reassured him.

Jeremy was beginning to understand the direction of his work. *His* work? The work that could not progress at a necessary pace without his contribution to it. To begin to understand the direction of his work was but part of his reorientation; *now* he started to understand its importance.

***

Charlie Wimpole sat down to compose what he would fax to KL within the given thirty minute slot. He liked to think he was an even-handed man. "A man of peace - unless provoked," he had often quipped. *This* did not feel even-handed; he doubted whether it was even professional; certainly, it had the potential for explosion. But what was the alternative? To do nothing was, in fact, to do something: to deny support to a desperate and decent woman; to align himself with Pontius Pilate.

Years later, he still wondered about that fax. Had Gerald intercepted it? Had Geraldine felt his advice to be inadequate? Had it been subject to technological mishap and never been delivered? The silence with which it was met would leave these questions unanswered, probably for ever. It would leave Charlie Wimpole as disorientated as those whom he had been asked to guide.

This House Believes .... .

One of the most memorable Union debates involving Jeremy and Anita that keen followers remembered was on a motion inspired by the writing of another Cambridge luminary, the novelist and essayist, E. M. Forster. "This House believes that to betray one's country, in order to save a friend, is an act of moral courage".

Jeremy had spoken for the motion; Anita had opposed.

His line of argument had called for a re-examination of the phrase, "one's country". Should where one was born but had never lived be termed "one's country"? Was it not possible to consider more places than one to be 'home' and, thus, "one's country"? What, precisely, does the word "country" mean? Is it merely a matter of geography or should its definition be more wide-ranging? Are large countries as singular in their identity as smaller ones? How far back into one's ancestry should one delve, in order to decide one's country of origin? Was he, for example, Malaysian or Chinese? If the latter, should he regard Hong Kong or Mainland China as *his*? If the former, why did he not speak Malay? Could one genuinely regard a country whose native language was foreign to be one's own?

The list of questions posed, with the intention of discrediting a phrase central to the motion, seemed as if it would never end. When it did, he had but laid his foundations. He next set about a philosophical and linguistic analysis of the word "betray". His purpose was to neutralise the emotive force of the term, which he recognised to be the most likely weapon of the opposition. Say it any way you like but "betray" is a word burdened with pejorative association. Lies may be white, cruelty can be kind, but betrayal wreaks of wrongdoing.

His strategy, thus far, had been to create uncertainty, to dislodge the firmly-set stones from which his listeners' walls of moral security were constructed. He wanted them to ask, "*could* the concept of national betrayal and all its attendant paraphernalia of guilt, accusation, and automatic condemnation, *in fact* be little more than the product of succeeding generations of governmental control over individual action?"

As he detected a wobbling of those walls and slight shifts in the position of their keystones, he moved to the final elements of the proposition: friendship and moral courage - two instantly appealing phenomena. This was where he hoped to add emotion to the mixture of philosophical challenge he had already prepared. To whom was friendship and moral courage not the two most significant factors within that state of being we call 'the human experience'? he had asked. He had not couched the question demandingly, as Churchill would have; nor had he charged it with dramatic, voice-quivering, emotion, as may a modern politician such as Tony Blair have opted for. His delivery had been understated. It could have been misinterpreted as being half-hearted, unconvinced, insincere. This had been the risk he took. So casual, so ordinary and everyday had been his tone, it was as if he were implying, "Do I really need to ask this question? Is not the answer self-evident?"

Having troubled his audience with doubts and made them revise long-held assumptions, this consolidation of something so certain, so fundamental, so simple restored their confidence in themselves. That there should be no doubt about this meant that there should be no doubt about what had preceded it. He had seen their quiescence. He allowed the thoughtful silence to settle a while and then, looking directly at them, he nodded his head in self-agreement, saying clearly, firmly, and with the only note of passion he had permitted himself throughout the speech, "I move." As he had lowered himself into his chair, the applause was spontaneous. Spontaneous, loud, and long.

Anita, predictably, had opposed not only the motion but the manner in which Jeremy had presented his case. Her delivery was volcanic. "Who could be so foolish as to be taken-in by such cheap sophistry?" she had hectored. Where Jeremy had sought to embrace his listeners, to draw them so close to himself they felt almost a part of him and of his thinking, Anita sought to distance them from her, shameful as they were. She was the scolding mother, seeking to show her children the error of their ways and to elicit apologies from them. Who in their right mind could possibly question their nationality? Next to one's own name it was the aspect of identity one knew best. The uneducated and the illiterate knew it; children only just able to speak knew it; those deemed by society to be insane knew it!

Part of her eruption had involved throwing into the air the pages upon which her speech was written. They rained-down upon the floor like the molten ash and rock from Vesuvius had once rained-down on unsuspecting Pompeii. The remainder of her speech had been delivered *ad lib*. It had been a bravura performance.

Of course, she had made maximum profit from her own national identity and from Cuba's history of struggle. "To raise issue over the philosophical existence of nationhood is to employ the centuries old casuistry of Imperialism! How easy history has shown it to be, this salving of a conqueror's conscience by questioning the integrity of borders and sovereignty!"

She had sensed a growing sympathy within her audience, as she moved towards the finale of her speech and her last words had been almost drowned by the cheers and applause they had engendered. "If you betray your country you are betraying *the best friend* you will ever have; what is more, you are betraying *every friend* you ever gave the name - and you will be friendless for the rest of your miserable existence!"

She had deliberately retained the singular form for her last word, highlighted by the dramatic pause immediately following what could have been her final phrase. "... your miserable existence!" had not been addressed to the audience but to Jeremy and her index-finger, pointing directly at him, singled him out - and his argument.

So sensational had the atmosphere within the Union been on that occasion that reports of it had escaped the confines of local press coverage. It was allocated space in a number of the nationals. It was in one of these national publications that those responsible for instructing Professor Tinniswood to supervise Jeremy's PhD had read the report.

Gerald had never thought he might, one day, thank Fothergill's for anything it had taught him. Self-prepared for university, wrongly and painfully beaten, patronised and marginalised throughout his two years there, his adult self had soon realised how foolish his teenaged self had been to become a means of helping to keep a dire establishment financially afloat.

As he dealt with the factory crisis to which he had been summoned, his mental paralysis lifted and he welcomed the return of his habitual competence. When he arrived home, he recognised that there was something more than the adrenaline of crisis-management that had enabled him to function. He had been to Fothergill's and he had survived the experience! No, that was not quite right. Fothergill's had taught him to survive; his capacity was more due to the school than to his own nature.

The incident at the factory had reactivated Gerald from his temporary torpor. He urged Geraldine to "snap out of it". He meant well (for he wished to share with her the glory of restored vigour that he was enjoying) but his urging was insensitive. How quickly we forget our visits to Hell, once we have located an exit.

Geraldine had sent her message to Charlie Wimpole. She had set in motion a sequence which she could not stop. Gerald, she knew, would be devastated to learn what she had done. Meanwhile, her only child had defied his parents - and she admired him for having done so. Geraldine Chan was out of sympathy with everything that defined her existence. Her only confidante was an Englishman, thousands of miles distant and ill-equipped to counsel her. Geraldine manoeuvred her way around Hell but could find no sign marked "Exit".

The pleasure of freedom Gerald had delighted in on the day he went to buy his mackintosh had been a unique few hours within the two-year-stretch he had served at Fothergill's. Those hours aside, the unjust beating he had suffered represented one of the few moments of relief from the tedious regimentation he had had to endure. Paradoxically, it was one of his most meaningful moments spent at this God-awful symbol of Britain's belief that all private enterprise should be applauded and upheld. Painfully buzzing buttocks had been better than the greater and longer-lasting pain of tedium, incompetence, and rank stupidity he had encountered every day of his time there. It had become necessary for him to devise stratagems to survive. These very same stratagems, once he had been summoned back to consciousness by his p.a., enabled him to re-engage. Slowly, his appetite returned, his sleep pattern re-established itself, he went every day to work, he commented on local issues, but he sedulously avoided the subject of their son.

Geraldine had no similar experience upon which to draw. She did not share the 'privilege' of having attended a two-by-four, back-of-the-book, tin-pot British (minor) Public School! She pinned her hopes to the fax-machine. She had nominated 6.00 – 6.30 p.m. as the time Charlie should send his response because she knew that Gerald would be in the shower at that time. It was part of his routine: back from work at 5.45, shoes removed and re-polished in readiness for the next day by 5.55, then straight to the shower; back downstairs at 6.40, refreshed and looking forward to a relaxed evening. She knew her letter would take several days to reach England and she realised that Charlie Wimpole would need time to consider his response. Nonetheless, from the day after she had posted her plea for help she positioned herself near to the fax machine as soon as Gerald went up for his shower. There, she stood guard until she heard his footsteps on the stair- case, casually flitting from it to other rooms with her feather duster, as she had done at this hour for as long as she could remember since she was first married. It pleased Gerald to think that he was to settle for the evening in rooms recently made ready for him.

Days passed this way. No response from Mr. Charlie. Had her letter fallen foul of the postal service? Was he no longer on the staff of Jeremy's old school? Had she made a fool of herself in Mr. Wimpole's eyes? Each evening, as her watch began, a fear that she may be caught by Gerald invaded the pit of her stomach. Each evening, at 6.32, that fear retreated, only to be replaced by a sense of having been abandoned; equally gut-gnawing, equally desolate. Meanwhile, she was still eating and sleeping far less than was good for her. If help from England was unavailing, it must be sought elsewhere. This, she recognised. She ought to make an appointment to visit a doctor.

***

Having pressed the 'send' button, Charlie Wimpole realised that he was committed. ("Should be committed!" an inner voice drolly muttered; the one that kept him on an even keel in times of difficulty.) He had been unsure and unhappy about this fax from the start. Good sense would have made him seek an independent view; the good sense he had in abundance, anyway, already told him what that independent view would be: "Don't interfere!"

There are times when our irrationality overwhelms us and we leap from an aeroplane without immediately opening the parachute, convinced that our sky-diving skills will guide us safely to the necessary opening point. Sky-diving skills we do not possess, in the first place!

As the paper was slowly chugging through, he *knew* he ought to press 'cancel'. But he didn't. The chugging gave way to a whirr. The original version softly settled on the tray. Thousands of miles away another piece of paper would, almost immediately, start its own chugging progress, as it slowly emerged from the belly of another fax machine, as if being born. It was now beyond his control.

Whilst Jeremy had not been an habitual correspondent, Charlie had received the occasional signal from him: early reports on how much he was enjoying Cambridge, a quick mention of Anita and of how stunning he found her to be, hopes of a good degree, following his first year exam. success, news that he was to begin work on his Doctorate. One way of extinguishing a fire, it is said, is to use more fire. Charlie was no scientist and he had no idea if such a theory held any credence but he felt compelled to test it. He wrote a letter to Jeremy:

Dear Jeremy,

So: how're matters Doctoral, m'boy? CW, here, lest you had not guessed!

I wonder if you could spare the time to give me a call? I have something you may be able to help me with (with which you may be able me to help!!)

Let me come clean: your mother has written to me (without your father's knowledge.) I am aware that there has been a family upset. As always, I am anxious to help, if I can, but reluctant to interfere. So what does Charlie W. do? Right first time, m'boy! Yes, I have replied to her; now I'm duplicating my interference by writing to you! I'm not at all sure this procedure features in the training manual!

Throw me a lifeline, if you can. If not, start to read the obituaries column!

Best, as ever,

Charlie Wimpole.

***

Coincidence is a curious characteristic of our lives. Only a few days after Charlie had written his letter to Jeremy, he received a letter postmarked Cambridge but the envelope looked altogether too formal for it to be a reply. It wasn't.

Dear Mr. Wimpole,

We understand that you were the Housemaster of a young man who has performed outstandingly as an undergraduate, here, and who is already embarked upon Doctoral research.

Of his academic standing, we harbour no doubts. He has also made quite a name for himself in the Union, where his intellectual ability has combined with innate powers of rhetoric to secure a considerable following. We congratulate you upon the part you must have played in nurturing this especial talent.

May I ask you to take a little time in providing us with some further information regarding Mr. 'Jeremy' Chan? To be specific: we are especially interested in your opinion regarding Mr. Chan's moral resilience and strength of character. For example, how would you anticipate him to respond to external pressures, to isolation, to danger, even?

This is part of a wider survey into our most able students that we are conducting and will offer us valuable information to add to an important research project the University is undertaking. Please do not fear that your observations (which will be, naturally, confidential to this office) could in any way impede the progress of your former pupil.

My kind regards and thanks in anticipation of your assistance.

Yours sincerely,

The letter had been signed by its author's p.a. and on his behalf. Its office of origin was that of The Deputy Vice-Chancellor. No longer Sir Edward Fitzmaurice, who had retired years before; the current incumbent was Sir William Abercrombie.

Had he not just become involved with the Chan family's affairs, Charlie would have known exactly what to do about this letter. He would have sent a copy to his Headmaster, seeking authorisation (or its inverse) to respond. Arriving when it had, it somehow acquired greater significance in his mind than it would ordinarily have done. Greater complexity. He changed its status from 'immediate action: HM' to 'pending'. He needed time to think.

Ménage A Trois.

"Is there anything you can't or don't eat, Jeremy?" Quentin and Hermione had invited their research assistant to dinner. They had become fond of him and found his company welcome in their tiny and isolated lab. area.

"I'm an international scoffer!" Jeremy responded. "Rice, chips, sweet potato: it's all good starch to me!"

"How accommodating!" Hermione riposted, "Oh, and thinking of accommodation, do remember to bring a wash bag to work with you, tomorrow. You *must* stay overnight. The spare room is all ready to receive!"

They drove him to their small home, guided him around the upstairs geography, which he had not ventured into on his previous visit, instructing him to come down whenever he was ready but by no later than 7.00. "There's plenty of hot water, if you want to wash all that lab. dust away before you eat. The shower room is yours. We have a little *en suite.*"

When Jeremy came downstairs, a gin and tonic was presented to him within seconds. A mild rouging of the cheeks indicated that Hermione had been testing botanicals for a little while. "Make yourself at home – or would you rather be my *sous-chef*? Do you enjoy cooking?"

"*Sous-chef* for me! Anita always cooks - cooked." He was wrong-footed for just a split second and then recovered, as if he had never faltered. "I *love* to cook; almost as much as I *love* to eat. It's the Asian in me!"

"Do you think there is a gender: race ratio, when it comes to cooking?"

"Oh, I meant *all* Asians love food. Those who can get it, of course." His comment had begun in high spirits but it ended on a note of social conscience. "I'm a privileged Asian. I do realise that."

That Hermione had an agenda for this evening she could not deny. That she should have reached it without effort both surprised and delighted her. "I'm a privileged European," she responded. "So, too, is Quentin. Cambridge is awash with inter-continental privilege." Her tone was light and whimsical. There was none of Anita's political engagement in what she said - or, rather, in the way she said it. "Come and chop some peppers; as the perfect hostess, I'll take-on the onions!"

And so they chopped and peeled, pared, sliced, and skewered. Hermione had decided upon *shish-kebab*, to be accompanied by cardamom-scented rice. This was to be preceded by a platter of crudités dipped into an eye-watering garlic mayonnaise. To follow would be freshly prepared fruit-salad, left to rest in maraschino just long enough to conjure fragrance but not so long as to numb the natural flavours.

"Of course, you realise that you're Quentin's second PhD student, only, don't you? I was his first but that was *years* ago."

Jeremy was not sure that this required a response, so he did not offer one.

"You may have wondered why it has been close on thirty years since he last supervised graduate research. Why he has remained in the quickly refurbished labs. he was offered, so many years ago. It's not that his work has been poor, you realise." An almost defensive comment, this. Unique in Jeremy's experience of Hermione, who was habitually measured in the way she conducted every aspect of her life.

He allowed eye-contact and a smile to answer the implied question. Yes, he had wondered but, no, he had never suspected underperformance to explain the anomaly that was Professor Quentin Tinniswood.

As on Jeremy's previous visit, the Professor did not appear until shortly before the meal was ready to serve. He offered no apology, seemed in no way flustered, took the drink his wife offered him and segued into conversation as if he had been with them for half-an-hour or more.

"Right!" said Hermione, "all's under control. Time for one more drink and then all will be ready."

Throughout the evening, Jeremy noted that Quentin was an excellent contributor to the conversation but never an initiator. That role was allotted to Hermione. She was like a ballet-dancer: skipping and leaping around her stage, changing pace and rhythm, producing pirouettes out of nowhere - and all quite effortlessly. Topics to address ranged from their work to books and articles they had read recently, plays or films they had seen, actions taken by the British and world-wide governments, ... It was an hypnotic evening.

Not until cheese and port was presented did Hermione become just slightly more focussed. "You were quite a performer at the Union, as an undergraduate," she noted, pinning Jeremy with her piercing blue eyes. Did not one of your famous tussles reach the notice of the national press?"

"Yes, I enjoyed the Union. And," the next yes was conveyed with amused self-deprecation, "yes, there was one occasion when journalists allowed themselves to get over-excited!"

"What were you debating? *Do* help yourself to celery; it's beautifully crisp." Her question might have been beautifully crisp, too, but she cushioned it with consummate expertise.

"Oh it was the old E.M. Forster chestnut about betraying one's country or one's friend."

"And you presented what line.....?" Again, her question was magnificently disguised, tossed-off as if she scarcely cared whether he answered or not, busying herself with biscuits to accompany the cheese.

"I took Forster's line."

"Out of belief or because you had been allocated that cause?" So casual, she might have been enquiring if he favoured black grapes or green, red wine or white, lemon or milk.

"I agree with Forster," he asserted and she noted that his casual tone had taken-on a more serious timbre. "There was a time when I knew who I was. Then I came to England. I am a genetic Oriental with a perfect English accent. The most significant years of my education have taken place in the West. Until just recently, I have been living with a girl located, geographically, just off the coast of the USA, and, ideologically, in the Moscow of Stalin, Lenin, and Khrushchev. My parents are shocked, not that I have been living with this girl outside of marriage but that she is outside of my race. *You* tell *me* who I am; what is *my nation!*" He paused, slightly conscious that he may have created a bit of a scene; that he may have transgressed the ground-rules of a dinner guest. "Rather like my eating habits, I'm International Man!" It had taken considerable effort but he had managed to re-establish a note of levity.

Hermione Carstairs smiled significantly at him. She then looked at her husband, paused momentarily, and with slick elision enquired, "Are we to be treated to your superbly created coffee, Quentin, and perhaps some *petits fours?*"

Honest & Of Good Report.

From: Charles Wimpole, B.A., M.Phil.

To: The Deputy Vice-Chancellor, Cambridge University.

Ref.: CHAN, Hong-Chun (Jeremy).

Status: STRICTLY CONFIDENTIAL.

Dear Deputy Vice-Chancellor,

With reference to your unexpected request for a character reference for one of our former pupils, Jeremy Chan, currently studying for a PhD in Chemical Engineering at Cambridge: I am authorised by my Headmaster to reassure you that we have no reason to believe that Mr. Chan is anything other than a first-rate young man. In well-wrought and Biblical phraseology, he is, to the best of our knowledge, "honest and of good report."

Yours sincerely,

Charles Wimpole.

Although he held the same office as its rambunctious first incumbent, Sir William Abercrombie was of a very different nature. Whereas Fitzmaurice may well have screwed-up Charlie's somewhat tartly expressed letter, propelling it to a waste-paper basket with a blunt curse to help it on its way, Sir William merely nodded, stretched for a manila folder, which already contained several sheets of paper, and carefully placed the letter atop the pile.

He then picked-up a Dictaphone. "Letter to Professor Quentin Tinniswood re his research assistant and PhD supervisee, Jeremy Chan. Dear Professor Tinniswood, my thanks for the invaluable information you have furnished me with, of late. All the signs are positive. I leave it to you to select the best route towards securing Mr. Chan's signature to The Official Secrets' Act. Yours, etc."

Root & Branch.

The main reason why Quentin Tinniswood had published only a relatively small body of academic work was that his forte lay in relating theory to practical application. It had been this talent that had been spotted early by the first Deputy Vice-Chancellor and it had been the cause of the then *Dr.* Tinniswood's unanticipated promotion to professorship.

The majority of his work had been for industry. Initially, with British companies but, subsequently, he operated within an international context. Sir Edward had been the principal manipulator of this shift. His view that there was far too much debating within the groves of academe expanded to the opinion that there was also "... too much thinking and insufficient doing!" To take-on centuries of philosophical tradition at one go was, even for his robust approach, a tall order. He recognised that such a venture would be quixotic. Thus, he selected Tinniswood as his micro-model of the academic future, as he envisaged it.

But Sir Edward, it will be recalled, worked not merely at the university. He worked, also, in government. The tree of government *we* see stands tall and graceful; but we do not see its root system, tendrils deep beneath the surface of the earth. They feed it and they support it. Without them the tree would wilt and topple. It was with this unglamorous network that Sir Edward was especially concerned. Governments are elected in accordance with the manifestos they present to the electorate. That is the tree onto which they are grafted. But, as parties in power change and fresh branches emerge, the root system remains intact. Hot war, cold war, or no war, the tree of government is watered and nurtured by information, much of it secret. The international work that Professor Tinniswood had been directed towards over the past four decades was, much of it, secret. Hermione Carstairs, the daughter of political commitment and intellectual freedom, had been his able assistant. Jeremy Chan, "International Man" by self-definition, was to be their heir.

***

Geraldine's appointment with the doctor was fixed. She deliberately avoided her more regular man, who was also something of a family friend. She desired independence of judgement and a degree of anonymity. Of course, she had not told Gerald of her intention. Her early evening vigils over the fax machine had been negated by the arrival of Charlie Wimpole's response. It was sympathetic; he avoided *parti pris*; there was nothing about it that could be considered compromising. All-in-all, it was thoroughly "English", both in content and in tenor. It did not, however, resolve her anxiety about their estrangement from Jeremy, nor did it restore her sleep and appetite. Reluctant to compound this form of infidelity, she shredded the fax and, with it, the interchange with Charlie.

Dr. Wendy Woo had been a recent recruit to the substantial KL practice that had provided the Chans with medical attention for many years. She had qualified at King's and Guy's in London and, thus, had more than a tangential understanding of Jeremy's role in Geraldine's current condition. "We're like trees;" she offered, "what you see of us is clearly identifiable: Oak, Elm, Ash, Larch, Spruce, or Beech. But you cannot see our roots, that underground system of nurture and support upon which what you see is wholly dependent."

They had been talking of the change that had taken place in Jeremy during the near-decade that he had spent in England. "You must understand that almost everything that has been contributing to his continued development over those years is quite different from what had nurtured him before. Physical geography gives KL and UK different climates; there are some trees common to both countries but they do not necessarily grow in the same way. You and your husband transplanted a sapling; had that sapling failed to recognise the cooler climate, the differing rain and sunshine patterns, changed soil conditions and so on, it would have become stunted, at best, perished, at worst. Like trees, human beings are used to growing where their seed germinated; they *can* and *do* adapt to being moved but, whilst they may *look* the same, the root ball has undergone significant change."

Contrived though the analogy was, it made sense. Geraldine understood the point that Dr. Woo was making and she respected the personal as well as the clinical expertise that the young doctor was bringing to bear upon the issue. It then occurred to Wendy that the wrong patient was seeking guidance. Gerald ought to be sitting in the chair she occupied! Tentatively, she raised this. "Of course, I don't know your husband, Mrs. Chan, but I know my father." Understanding had been both offered and received.

Geraldine went on to explain all about Fothergill's and how Gerald had returned to KL, following his time in England, as culturally traditional as he had left. This begged the question of

Jeremy's transformation.   Again, the young medic. sought clarification by analogy. "It is not just the *global* climate that has changed during the last half-century, Mrs. Chan. Neither KL nor UK is, now, as it was, then The expectations of and from my/Jeremy's generation are different from those of yours and your husband's."

Geraldine could not stop herself. "To assume I share my husband's views is to assume too much, Doctor!" As she heard her own words bouncing off the consulting-room walls, she was shocked. But it had been said.

"I stand appropriately corrected." There was no offence in Dr. Woo's tone; just acknowledgement of an evident truth.

A naturally polite woman, Geraldine was mortified by her aggressive tone – and not least because of its implied criticism of Gerald's outlook. "Please forgive me, I'm not myself," she stammered.

"Nothing to forgive;" Wendy reassured her, "to assume husband and wife share all opinions is to embrace what my professor used to call 'The Happy Families Fallacy'! It was a lightness of touch which rescued the consultation. Following a well-timed pause, Dr. Woo asked, "Would you say that your differing attitudes have contributed to your condition?"

"Common sense tells me that they must have – but my husband, too, felt as I do. At first."

Although Geraldine's habitual equipoise had been swiftly restored, Dr. Woo reflected, "This woman needs help." She prepared to advise her patient how best to proceed. "May I propose a course of action?" she asked. Geraldine looked at her, expectantly, by way of affirmation. "If you do not restore a normal pattern of eating and sleeping, your physical health will deteriorate. It would seem that the key to this lies in your *mental* state of health. There *is* medicine that I shall prescribe, but the current thinking is that a form of cognitive therapy is advisable, also."

"I am willing to try the medication, which I will be able to hide from Gerald but I would imagine that the therapy would be more difficult to disguise."

"Your husband's involvement in the cognitive therapy *is* considered to be a positive aspect of its effectiveness."

"Impossible!" On this point, Geraldine was adamant.

"I have to warn you that, whilst the medication rarely has unpleasant side-effects, it *does* take a while to become effective."

"Never the less, I shall take my chances with the tablets, alone." The two women's eyes met. Dr. Woo typed-in to her computer the requisite prescription, pressed the print button, signed the paper which emerged, and handed it to her patient. Mechanical though these actions were, they were executed with a sensitive deftness.

"I wish you well, Mrs. Chan," she said. Not out of professional habit but with a half-tone of personal involvement. "I *do* understand your situation," she added, a discernible opacity clouding her eyes, as she shook hands and closed the door. After all, she too had made the journey Westwards, once.

A Red-Letter Day.

Realpolitik had been mixed with Anita's milk from the day of her birth. Had she not grown into an articulate and skilful exponent of it, the prospect of two subsidised years in the world of Western academic freedom would never have been contemplated by the State of Cuba. The events following the surprise visit of Jeremy's parents had prompted her to reflect. Did she love Jeremy enough to fight for their relationship's restoration? Indeed, did she *love* Jeremy, period? Did not this situation raise more important issues than the purely personal? Should she shrug her shoulders, walk away and move on, or should she engage?

The more thought she gave it, the more outraged she became. To be embroiled-by-association in an issue fuelled by so many assaults upon her abiding principles demanded an uncompromising response. Her pen hovered over a sheet of paper. *Jeremy*, she began, dismissing *Dear* as petit-bourgeois hypocrisy. She had seriously considered *Comrade* as a suitable form of address but, again, she refused to allow convention to compromise candour.

Jeremy,

You have allowed yourself to become the victim of paternalistic imperialism, from which you have, in a cowardly manner, run-away, rather than supporting the universal struggle, which was your fundamental human duty.

Every authoritarian act that is perpetrated against a fellow mortal diminishes the dignity of all Humankind. It is food for the maw of tyranocracy! You, personally, are guilty of having brought delay to the day that shall surely come: the day of social, financial, personal, and political justice.

Shame on you!

Anita del Azura.

She did not know Jeremy's new address, thus she sent her letter *c/o The Chemical Engineering Department*, from where he retrieved it. Ever since "Debacle Day", as he whimsically called it, Jeremy had been irked by an underlying feeling of guilt, regarding Anita. True, she had exhibited no sympathy for him over either his parents' unexpected arrival or, indeed, their equally unexpected departure. She had been too preoccupied with what she considered to be the political ramifications of the event to lend it the perspective of Cultural Relativism. To her, *all* invasion deserved resolute counter-attack, designed to repulse. Negotiation was no better than collaboration. None the less, the breadth of view Anita's political blinkers denied her was accessible to Jeremy, courtesy of Charlie Wimpole *et al.* He recognised how galling the episode must have been to her and how let-down by him she must have felt. He did not agree with her but he understood. It was this that had made the last couple of months' estrangement uncomfortable for him.

Her letter changed all that. No longer could 'Latin spontaneity' excuse her. This was not a reaction but a response. It had been drafted, edited, proofed, and posted, at leisure. What she had written, she had meant. Whilst he was out of sympathy with his parents, he could not embrace Anita's doctrinaire dogma. He lacked her commitment to the cause of liberty. Then, suddenly, he recognised an essential truth about himself: he lacked *all* commitment. His research with Professor Tinniswood was the closest to commitment he had ever felt.

He would not reply to Anita. He would not actively seek a reconciliation with his parents. In another's phrase, he felt *free at last*!

On The Dotted Line.

Whilst Sir William's letter had been addressed to Quentin, the task was immediately passed to Hermione. She would handle it so much better, he felt.

She handled it with remarkable ease. Resurrecting their previous conversation about the celebrated Union debate, they came to agree that to feel *no* sense of Nationhood was merely the reverse face of the coin whose obverse made its national identity evident. If his signature to The Official Secrets' Act was essential to the continuation of his work with Professor Tinniswood, he could see no reason to withhold it.

***

Geraldine signed the back of her prescription and collected her medication. That she needed to address her current state of health she understood; that this would be but a temporary solution to her real problem was equally clear to her. Re-establishing contact with her son was essential. She would not recover properly until it had been achieved.

***

As soon as he received the signed, witnessed, and dated documentation from Quentin, Sir William swung into action. "Would you put a call through to the Home Secretary, please?" he asked his p.a., settling into his well-upholstered desk chair and nestling the telephone receiver to his ear.

***

Understanding the Chemistry upon which he, Quentin Tinniswood, and Hermione Carstairs were concentrating their attentions, Jeremy had formulated a range of possible practical applications to which their findings could well be put. It pleased him to think that his efforts would contribute to the betterment of struggling lives. However, such applications had never formed part of any discussion he had ever engaged in with either Quentin or Hermione. Not until he was asked to sign The Official Secrets' Act did it occur to him to ask either of them to what practical ends *they* were looking.

As is so often the case in the worlds of Politics and Intelligence, the answer came in the form of an acronym: ***SPA*** - redolent of health and well-being, it seemed to Jeremy.

***

My very dear, dear Jeremy,

We were wrong. Wrong to visit unannounced; wrong to steal away in the middle of the night; wrong to make such unreasonable demands. What we are left with is wrong, as well: the break-down of what ought to be a wonderful relationship. In its place we have emptiness; utter emptiness that never goes away.

We are different from you, your father and I. We were brought-up differently; what was expected of us was different from what you want for yourself. Your father's years at Fothergill's did not give him the same outlook as your own schooldays did. He spent his time in England with only one plan in mind: to return home, empowered with useful knowledge, and to resume a way of life he had been used to. He considered it his duty. Duty was instilled into our generation. It has, in some ways, played a vital part in our lives, giving us determination in difficult times. But it has also enslaved us.

I write to you, Jeremy, not out of duty but out of love. Please, please, reply. Just to hear from you is all I ask.

Your loving Mother, who longs to be called Mom, once more.

Geraldine addressed, sealed, and stamped the envelope. As Anita had done, she directed it to the Chemical Engineering Department. She went out, especially, to post it. Delay may result in dither and dither may lead to loss of nerve. She felt the urge to act.

Better Lethe Than Styx?

"Socrates was forced to drink Hemlock. Alexander Litvinenko was fed radioactive Polonium-210. Both knew too much; both had to die for the knowledge they possessed. The State considered it too dangerous to let them live. That's what 'Intelligence' is: knowledge that can both benefit and destroy The State. Those in possession of it must be controlled. Death is the ultimate control."

Hermione was warming to her theme. She had a personal interest in the ephemeral relationship between Intelligence and The State. The father she had never met had disappeared in Spain. No body for her mother to bury; no grave for her to visit. He had sent one letter, heavily censored, and that was the last of him. He was reported "Missing, presumed dead." No personal effects had ever been retrieved. None of the few books he had taken with him; no diary; no I.D. of any sort, no mementos. This had been the paternal void with which Hermione had grown-up.

"State Secrets have existed since the beginning of organised society and they will exist until its end. Of that truth we need harbour no doubts. The question is as it has always been: how best may those secrets be protected? One man is given to expounding in public, another defects to a country not wholly in accord with the politics of his own; both represent a de-stabilising threat; each must be eliminated. We oppose such action on the part of others, yet we practise it ourselves. The Conspiracy Theory is not the invention of the modern world. Nor is it a theory, alone. Human beings *do* conspire; *have* conspired; *will* conspire. Were it in your power to do so, how might *you* eliminate the threat of spilling Intelligence without spilling blood?"

The conversation had been initiated by Hermione at Quentin's bidding. Their research into the properties of certain chemical substances in combination with each other was moving forwards and Jeremy was growing increasingly intrigued by the proposed application to which their discoveries might be put. Although he had signed The Official Secrets document with an alacrity born of little enquiry, he had subsequently started to give it increasing thought. He had put his question directly to Quentin, recently, only to receive a bland generalisation by way of response. He had come to expect a degree of obtuseness from the professor; not so from his wife, whose cobalt clear eyes had signalled a proactive nature from the first time they had magnetised his attention.

"Well, if the one possessing the knowledge is to be allowed to live, the only option is to eliminate the knowledge, itself."

"Precisely."

"Hypnotism?"

"Hypnotism's too random. Even assuming its efficacy, how could one guarantee someone with the necessary skill would be instantly available when required?"

"Brain washing?" This was said slightly tongue-in-cheek. Jeremy felt he was teetering on the margins of spy-thrillers and he expected Hermione to echo his amusement.

"Now, *that's* a more promising track to pursue!" At first, he thought she was making fun of him. He had noticed how she enjoyed mild mockery; Quentin was her habitual target. But no accompanying laughter followed. "What might be the challenges of such a process do you imagine?"

He had not been anticipating this throw-away suggestion becoming a theme to develop and he had not given it any serious consideration. Hermione allowed the silence which followed to persist. Suddenly, he felt like a callow student in a supervision, his teacher challenging him to analyse a problem and to produce a solution.

"Time?" he proffered, hesitantly.

"Good! Traditional approaches to the process popularised through the phrase 'brain-washing' take time. They also share the inconvenience of hypnotism. Other challenges?"

Jeremy recognised that Hermione considered this to be central to the germ of her original observations concerning Socrates and Litvinenko. "Let's crystallise the problem we are addressing: an individual is in possession of certain secret knowledge; circumstances suddenly threaten to compromise its secretive status. In an ideal world, what needs to happen next – assuming our specified individual holds the answer to our conundrum, *and* we have eliminated assassination from our options?"

Jeremy's mind moved into chess default mode. He wanted to offer the answer that Hermione, herself, was nursing. He tested various options in his mind before deciding to capitalise upon the encouragement his gambit of time had enlisted. "Immediacy," he eventually concluded, dwelling on each of the word's five syllables, as if it were indeed a chess-piece that he was reluctant to let go of, lest he wish to change his move.

Hermione nodded, noting that the threat of compromise was, indeed, likely to increase with time and, thus, the inverse was likely to be true. He acknowledged that his move had not endangered any of his other pieces but neither had it manoeuvred him into a challenging position. He was now totally focussed. "To keep the knowledge and the individual safe, simultaneously," he mused. "*Why* is the individual in danger? Because knowledge he (or she) has is wanted by someone else; remove the knowledge; remove the danger. Both achieved!" Hermione's eyes were positively atwinkle. She had enjoyed witnessing the process by which Jeremy had reached this point.

"Remove the knowledge, *yes*! But *how*? And with *what* attendant danger?

Hermione's apostrophising was the product of enthusiasm, rather than of frustration. She recognised that Jeremy could see his way to endgame; he simply had to make the apposite moves. "A product needs to be developed which destroys designated knowledge at will, whilst all else remains intact."

His final word had scarcely been enunciated when Hermione's first overlapped it. "A process known as *SPA: Specified Personal Amnesiant* !"

Taking Stock.

Jeremy was touched by the simple sincerity of his mother's letter. He was also aware of the anguish it would have caused her to write solo and, thus, without his father's knowledge. He had long-since recognised in her a fellow spirit *manqué* and he had been well aware, all those years ago when there had been such a farrago over his A level choices, that her signature had been mere tokenism. He would not say that she was jealous of the freedoms he enjoyed (jealousy was not in Geraldine's nature) but he did recognise that she had been, privately, in sympathy with him then and that she was, essentially, in sympathy with him now.

The question was: how best to react to her letter? A reply was out of the question. Even were he to type the envelope, a letter addressed to her alone and posted in Britain would arouse his father's suspicions. A fax would be equally risky. He could call her on her cell-phone at a time he knew she would be alone but the prospect of a disembodied conversation within the existing context was unappealing and fraught with the potential for disaster. Silence, however, might seem to betoken callous disregard.

How best to respond to his mother's letter was but one of the issues that troubled Jeremy's thoughts, just now. He was still reeling from his discovery regarding SPA. Was the irony of his original assumption about this healthy-sounding acronym accidental or calculated, he wondered.

Hermione's lecturette concerning the preferable river of Hades to navigate had manoeuvred him back into Debating mode. At the time, he had elected not to respond but Hermione was too bright and too realistic to consider his silence to betoken consent. She knew that her deconstruction had created an electrical charge which had temporarily stunned her husband's research assistant.

"This House favours engineered memory loss over termination" may offer discursive opportunities to an aspiring hero of the Union but, in reality, it was too pat by far. "Any state is better than death" had about it the rallying ring of the rhetorician. Its lack of minutiae, however, called it into severe question.

Many questions, in fact. They flooded Jeremy's waking thoughts and his dreams. Is being a water-boarded prisoner in Guantanamo Bay better than death? Is persisting in a near vegetative state? What about a lifetime's solitary confinement in Spandau? Painting with a broad brush may be bold but it lacks finesse.

What *is* 'life'? More than an uninterrupted heart-beat, surely. We are an accumulation of everything we have been, everything we have done, everything we have known. Diminish any part of that and diminish 'life'. Even a computer, once a file is deleted, retains its cookies. Human beings *must* hold the right to, at least, emulate a computer! And the potential for error. For more than the designated data to be dissolved .... To Jeremy, this was more than alarming. And to have become party to it left him feeling physically nauseous. "This is no anodyne *Specified Personal Amnesiant*; this is crude amputation!" He could hear the response to this conclusion to a speech – an audience brought to shocked silence and challenged to disagree, if it dared.

But he was not drafting a speech. He was no longer a commentator but, rather, a contributor. *His* work had enabled SPA to develop far enough to attract the interest of the Government's custodians of Intelligence. *He* had put his signature to a legally-binding document. - And then, suddenly, a thought struck him: "*I* hold information that may be considered dangerous, should it be revealed. Could it possibly be that, ultimately, it is intended that my involvement in this development should be more than academic?" He felt the sweat cascade down his torso, chilling uncomfortably as it dribbled into his waistband.

Decisions, Decisions.

Following days of prevarication, Jeremy decided to text his mother. This approach offered numerous advantages: she would know that he was open to further contact; brevity was appropriate; Geraldine's privacy would be maintained. *Mom, letter received, understood, and its spirit embraced. We will find a way. Love, Jeremy.* Once he had pressed 'send', he felt so much better. Not the relief of a guilty conscience cheaply salved, but the sense of a wrong beginning to be righted.

It had been a Friday upon which both Hermione had addressed him and he had picked-up his mother's letter from the Department pigeon-holes. His text had been sent on the Sunday morning. This had left the remainder of Sunday to think about SPA.

Nothing about him suggested that Quentin Tinniswood was a bad man. Nothing he was known to have worked on and developed had done anything other than to enhance human existence. Without doubt, he was unworldly; and yet he had contributed to the world's well-being in a more direct and applicable way than almost any of his immediate contemporaries at the university. To rise against him may have been Jeremy's instinct but the weekend gave him time for greater wisdom.

Hermione, on the other hand, he recognised as no *ingénue*. Firstly, the research student, then the wife, always the lab. assistant, she deliberately made her function enigmatic. Without a doubt, however, she had inherited her father's 'political commitment' gene. Is political commitment to be held in suspicion? Anita del Azura would be very clear in response to this question. And he had admired Anita *because* of her political radicalism. Literature had embraced Mr. Carstairs' cause. Decades of criticism had left Orwell and Auden unscathed, on that front. Hemingway was admired, even by his detractors. "Better to embrace *something* than never to embrace at all" was another of the undergraduate Union motions that echoed in Jeremy's memory.

"Why me?" – the question that Jeremy inevitably reached. His ensuing responses were not comforting. Decades of fitting-in. Jeremy Chan: Chameleon Man. To blend, to merge, to assimilate. To become acceptable; to be khaki. "I have neutralised myself," he admitted. *Will you speak for or against the motion? I don't mind.*

Now he understood Hermione's acuity. Was there any trace of Jeremy Chan that signalled "belonging"? *None!* Not to belong is not to care. It offers the autonomy of an Emperor - or the servitude of a pawn.

Irresolute.

She could not help herself. "He's been in touch!" she blurted-out to her husband during one of their customary, silent evening meals. "I've had a text."

Gerald looked at her. He then re-addressed his noodles. Silence obtained. Chop-sticks clattered against porcelain. And again. And again. And again. He pushed his emptied bowl aside and helped himself to another cup of tea. He sipped and he swallowed; sipped and swallowed again. She looked at him, seeking a sign. None appeared.

***

Following the weekend, Jeremy determined to arrive at the labs. neither earlier nor later than usual. He stowed his jacket, swapping it for his white lab. coat. He then made his way to his station. Quentin and Hermione were always in earlier. They, too, were in position.

His greeting was as ordinary as he could manufacture. He logged-on and called-up the relevant file. The next half-an-hour passed in silence.

It was Quentin who broke it. Quentin, who normally merely observed and tabulated, prior to giving considered assessment. "I understand you had a chat with Hermione on Friday," was all he said.

"Yes, indeed," replied Jeremy, reluctant to reveal through phrase or through tone anything more than the factual.

"She introduced you to the possible longer-term applications of our research," the professor ventured, more as a question than a statement.

"She did." Jeremy was determined not to reveal his hand any sooner than he must.

"Do you have thoughts?" Quentin asked.

"Yes, I do," fenced Jeremy.

"And .... ?" The elongated enunciation, followed by the unfilled space, was an invitation to Jeremy. He chose silence.

Quentin was wise enough to let the matter drop, whilst exchanging significant glances with Hermione.

It was a leaden morning. And a leaden afternoon.

***

Gerald took his napkin to his lips and patted them, meticulously. It had been something Mr. Fothergill had been especially insistent upon. He folded the napkin with punctilious care, even though he knew that Geraldine would put it directly into the wash. He sipped another cup of tea, slowly and methodically, then he stacked his used crockery, once more in Fothergill's fashion, and left it for Geraldine to clear.

"Thank you, Geraldine," he proffered, with his habitual courtesy. "Most pleasant." He then left the room and moved to his study.

"Fool! Fool!" Geraldine scolded herself. The moment she had opened her mouth to say that Jeremy had made contact, she recognised her error. Too late.

***

Monday's pattern was copied on Tuesday and on Wednesday. Quentin threw-out the occasional line of conversation. Jeremy let it fall short. Hermione observed with detached, feline attention.

***

Breakfast for Gerald and Geraldine was rarely an opportunity for conversation. Changes to their habitual routines were exchanged. No more. Toast was crunched. Tea was slurped. Gerald set-off for the factory. Geraldine cleaned and tidied. The day slowly unfolded. Monday had been no exception. Breakfast on Tuesday, Wednesday, Thursday, and Friday was an even bleaker occasion than normal. The intervening dinners were no more convivial.

At last, Geraldine ventured a question. "Are you going to ask me why he texted?" She had selected dinner to ask her question; it offered Gerald less opportunity to escape it.

"Very well. Why?"

"He is a loving, caring child."

"And what, precisely, lies behind that observation?"

Geraldine recognised that she had become engaged in a form of tug-o'-war. Gaining ground was the object of the contest. There would be no exchange of blows. Each would dig-in, hold firm, hope to wear the other down, and to vanquish.

***

Hermione broke the impasse. "You have qualms," she asserted in a manner he felt he could not ignore.

"It raises complex moral questions, certainly," he replied.

"Our every action, as human beings, raises moral questions, Jeremy." Her tone was not exactly impatient. More patronising. She wanted to minimise, to diminish, his distaste for SPA. As she spoke, he tried to avert her gaze. Those willow-pattern blue eyes might be his undoing, he knew. They anaesthetised him.

"How would we test it?" he asked. "More specifically, on whom?"

"Our task is not to test." More a mantra than a comment, this was Hermione Carstairs' formula for distancing herself from the actuality of her work. Jeremy could not decide which he found the more shocking: her involvement in the programme or her denial of its possible consequences.

A Most Unlikely Activist.

As a child, Quentin Tinniswood had been unexceptional. The third of five children, he had succeeded in finding stratagems for 'disappearing', content that his elder and younger siblings should attract his parents' attention. Unlike his brothers and sisters, he seemed never to hurt himself, nor to give way, noisily, to pangs of hunger. Although extremely inquisitive, he preferred to discover how and why for himself, rather than to demand explanations, whereas they, like chicks in a nest, were almost always squawking for attention. He adapted readily to school. No seeker-out either of friendship or of recognition, he acquired adequate quantities of both, without drawing attention to himself. He yearned for no more. Chicken Pox and Measles, the occasional grazed knee, minor losses and squabbles: he experienced a 'normal' childhood but, essentially, an invisible one.

His years of secondary education maintained much the same momentum. The requisite exams. were studied for and passed without trauma; he gained selection for B Teams in most sports – perhaps significantly, he was most adept at Cross-Country Running. He enjoyed and was successful at Chess but, for mental stimulation, he preferred crosswords. Being more mathematical than literary, he would no doubt have transferred his puzzle allegiances to Sudoku, had he been several generations younger. He generated little fuss about his preparation for a scholarship to Cambridge, which he secured with apparent ease. There, he was successful but uninterested in competing for the glittering prizes that could have been his were he to have wanted them. Whilst he did not manage a Starred First, the quality of his 'finals' scripts found no difficulty in securing the necessary financial backing for his move into Doctoral research. Three quietly studious years passed. They were followed by others, during which he gained his minor reputation for meticulously clear, accurate, applicable work.

Because he lacked both personal and professional flamboyance, aspiring research students never sought him out to supervise their work, nor did his seniors consider him to be sufficiently inspiring to encourage approach. Then, to his surprise but by no means his opposition, Hermione Carstairs had been propelled in his direction. No one had been surprised, three years later, that she emerged with her Doctorate but the engagement ring had been a stone to cause ripples of comment over the surface of the comparatively still waters of the Chemical Engineering Department. She was known to have a personality as brilliant as her blue eyes. A *much* racier match than they had imagined for their tweed-jacketed colleague, Quentin Tinniswood.

Further incident-empty years passed. No children were produced, but a number of noteworthy, if understated, papers, books, and projects were. It was at this juncture that Sir Edward Fitzmaurice had made his unanticipated approach, from which Professorship and independent, though constrained, lab. space had emerged.

No biography of Quentin Tinniswood ever having been deemed appropriate, Jeremy was unaware of most of his ex-supervisor's life-story, save for knowing that Hermione had once also been his only other supervisee, that they were childless, and that they were devoted to one another, both as husband and wife and as work colleagues. Because she was far more naturally communicative, he did know a little of Hermione's story. Political consciousness had suggested a bridge between Anita del Azura and her long-dead father, about whom she eventually came to tell him a little.

Sketchy though the details were, it was a Romantic tale of idealistic heroism and intrigue, given that her father's body had never, to the best of her knowledge, been found. Certainly never returned. Her telling of the story was enhanced, not merely by her narrative skill but also by the controlled emotional impact conveyed through the extraordinary eyes that had fascinated him from their very first meeting. Fascinated him so much that he could well imagine the effect they had had upon Quentin, years ago. Perhaps he, too, had been anaesthetised. Perhaps he still was. Perhaps this explained so much that had been left unsaid.

Jeremy was quite an authority on Quentin's published canon. Until recently, he had had no reason to believe that there was any other. Only since he had been introduced to the SPA project had he recognised that there must have been work of a similarly secretive provenance. His initial disbelief that this mild-mannered, unassertive man should have been involved in a form of espionage, probably for years, had taken a while to dissolve. But he came to recognise the reality of it: Quentin Tinniswood's very reticence was his most effective cover. "Identify the man by colour, and khaki comes to mind. Khaki, the very colour I recently allotted to my own emergent identity." For Jeremy, this was not a comforting parallel to contemplate. He had never before dwelt upon the paradox that passivity can be the most effective form of action. He had never before envisaged becoming the third point in a spy triangle. He assumed that a combination of undemonstrativeness and love had propelled Quentin into this unlikely region. Jeremy may well be fascinated by Hermione but he did not love her. Was he, he wondered, as neutral as the professor, or did he carry stronger pigments with which he may paint? That he should find himself posing the question indicated that he did. But he needed to locate them. Already, he realised that to prove himself more partial than he had seemed; to become more deliberate than diffuse; to exhibit resistance: these would be steps along a path laced with tripwires, whose intention was to fell him.

Back To School (i).

Dear ex-Wimpoleite,

In recognition of his fifteen years devoted service and upon the occasion of his retirement, we invite you to celebrate Charlie Wimpole's Housemastership. This will take the form of buffet luncheon, to be held on Saturday, June 22nd, starting at Noon. We do hope that you will be able to join us. The letter had gone on to outline arrangements for a presentation and proposals for those who planned to make a weekend of the event.

Jeremy had not been one for returning to his old school. This had been directed by no particular animus, rather it was another aspect of that detachment that had resulted in his current difficulties. Charlie Wimpole had been very good to him during his five years as a pupil. And by no means merely to him. The man's reputation rested upon the care and attention he had attempted to lend all his charges. He deserved acknowledgement and Jeremy decided to accept the invitation.

He then wondered whether his two especial school friends, Tom and Harry, would be attending. A slightly remote but sincere link had been maintained, since they had all left school and headed-off in differing directions. Tom had gone to Exeter, Harry to York. The geographic triangulation had not made for close contact. But each had managed to keep-up with the other via the increasing accessibility of contemporary social networking. Tom had taken an Upper Second in English and then moved "into the City" as did so many of his generation. Harry, waggish as ever, had rejoiced in his "Desmond", teasing elderly relatives into guessing the 2:ii code. He had studied Sociology and always maintained that it was his excessive interest in the practical aspect of the subject that had resulted in his modest academic achievement. His ready wit, silken style, and effortless charisma had landed him a job with a distinctly "up-market" Estate Agency. A firm that only sold properties with thousands of acres attached to them.

Jeremy's dalliance with Anita del Azura had attracted the interest of both his friends and had prompted squalls of sub-undergraduate banter which, had she been aware of it, would have ignited Anita into a rage against the puerile privilege of private education. Always more understated than either of his friends, though drawing upon his natural inclination towards mild satire, Jeremy had posted a number of waspish observations about their own extra-curricular sorties. Thus, a decade or more since they had first met, much the same cut-and-thrust of Junior Dorm. life shaped their relationship.

Are you going to Charlie W's bash? signalled Jeremy to both Tom and Harry. *Definitely*, responded Tom; *Should be a laugh – c u there* was Harry's slightly sassier return.

All of this had taken place in April. It had been some three or four months since Gerald and Geraldine's surprise visit and a few weeks had followed since Hermione's revelation about SPA. Might it be worth waiting until late June to take any further steps in either direction? To talk with Tom and Harry – perhaps, even, with Charlie Wimpole?

Sharpened caution enabled him to continue his work quietly and without remonstrance. He recognised, however, that his mother's cause demanded attention. Happily, the anticipated School Reunion offered him an oblique approach.

Dear Mom and Dad,

Guess what? I'm going back to school in a couple of months. Charlie Wimpole is retiring and there is to be a big gathering. Both Tom and Harry have said that they will go and it will be great to see them both, after too many years without meeting-up.

Is there anything worse than losing contact, would you say?

Love,

Jeremy.

It could not be considered a fulsome piece of correspondence but it was contact. He had drawn upon his debating skills to conclude it upon an invitation to respond. His mother was released from the need for subterfuge. His father was offered the choice of regarding this as the first blink or of exercising continued obduracy. Jeremy was satisfied by his efforts.

What had started out as something of a duty response became an anticipated pleasure. The sight of first year undergraduates frolicking in the delights of a Cambridge summer reminded him of his own not-long-out-of-school days. They, in turn, took him back to a distinctly more innocent past. To pack an overnight bag; to catch the train; to leave Cambridge behind, as he headed south, was to cast-off cares. Even though he knew that he would be making the reverse journey on Sunday afternoon.

His taxi drove through the well-remembered gates and swept up the gently curving drive, stopping outside the main entrance, which had already been transformed into a Registration Point. It was a beautiful day. The sunshine melted the austerity of the Victorian Gothic facade, red brick acquiring an almost Cotswold-stone-like honeyed softness; machicolations and pointed arches absorbing an edge-blurring kaleidoscope of hues and shades. Well-spaced trees offered shelter for those who sought it, dappling the manicured lawns with lozenges of balletic light. Several gently-billowing mini-marquees occupied strategic positions, offering sustenance and refreshment. The whole scene conjured-up something of a hybrid between Edwardian Garden Party elegance and a Romantic notion of the French Headquarters before Agincourt. "Et in Arcadia ego", muttered Jeremy, with rather more mirth than sincerity.

Signed-in and labelled, he moved towards the throng. The afternoon became everything he had hoped it would be. Charlie Wimpole was in fine form, remembering everyone (and, often, more than each cared to recall), basking in a rare combination of good weather, good memories, and good catering. His reunion with Tom and Harry was much more emotional than he had anticipated. Both sets of parents were also there; they stood back to allow their children space and then, themselves, moved-in to embrace. He had spent so many half-terms with them that they had long-since considered him to be (almost) their own.

"Are you returning to Cambridge, tonight?" Charlie almost whispered into Jeremy's ear during a momentary lull.

"No. I'm going to catch-up with Tom and Harry, this evening. My train's at 3.00 tomorrow afternoon."

"Might lunch be a possibility?"

"I think Brunch with the boys is more than likely. Mid-day drinks?"

"You know your way. Any time after twelve."

"I'll be there."

He had not planned but he had hoped. He *knew* that Charlie Wimpole was the closest he could come to discretion. What he didn't know was that his ex-Housemaster had been asked to provide the assurance which had activated Sir William's 'go-ahead'.

Boys' Night Out.

Whilst it had been wonderful to exchange inconsequentialities with so many during the afternoon, Jeremy had not been disappointed when it came time for the Presentation, itself a subtle signal to suggest that the show was winding-up. His plan to retreat with Tom and Harry for the evening was in place. All three had booked rooms at the same gastro-pub, sufficiently far removed from the immediate locality to make it unlikely that they would be intruded upon by unanticipated others.

It was an evening mainly devoted to nostalgia. "Do you remember when?" "What about the time that?" "Of course, Charlie pretended to be clueless, but ... ." It was a couple of hours before they reached as far as their leaving; another was taken over the three years that had followed. Finally, "So, what's what, these days, then?" was reached.

"The City's *sooo* knife-edge," Tom enthused. He, too, had become sharper. Once, dreamily, he had delighted in *Gatsby*, *Jane Eyre*, *Streetcar*, Keats and Emily Dickinson. Futures were his current crush. "Step onto the trading floor half-an-hour before the markets close and *smell* the testosterone!" he dramatised, inhaling deeply, like an addict snorting a line of cocaine. It was a rather unappealing exhibition.

"What about you, Harry? Are you a bottom-line jock, too?" asked Jeremy, combining mild mockery with a sense of comic unlikelihood.

Surprisingly, Harry did not release the anticipated self-deriding laughter. "There's nothing wrong with making money, Jezza. Why dis it?" His tone was that of a genuine apologist. It took a moment for Jeremy to realise he was in earnest. Harry, who had kicked, batted, and tackled his way through school, before drinking and dancing his way through university, had become a profit-motive proselyte. "Walk around some of these estates I sell and you realise what *real* money means. *I'll* never have a bank balance anywhere near it but I'm in awe." Jeremy could not recall Harry being in awe of anything nor anyone. He could not recall Harry having access to such vocabulary.

"Let's cut to Jezza Chan, brain-bracer extraordinaire!" scoffed Tom, pretending to focus a hand-held movie camera. "So, soon-to-be-Doctor Chan, how *does* a Cambridge Starred First earn a crust? What new method of mass-destruction are you working on, as you make your way to Nobel Laureateship?" The words might have been bitter, dismissive, accusatory. How Jeremy wished they had been. But their wit and levity denied the possibility that he may be involved in anything so nugatory.

"I'm poised to be party to a sale of far greater magnitude than either of you," would have been laughed-off as comic one-upmanship, had he said it. But he didn't. He didn't say anything. He merely pushed a cold chip around his discarded plate, looking like a lost little Malaysian boy in an alien land. Both Harry and Tom were in too high spirits to notice his silence, let alone his look.

He had hoped for more of this evening. For a clarification that would enable him to put Charlie Wimpole's evident concern to rest, the following afternoon. When it came time to say goodnight, he knew precisely how they spent their working lives; they had no inkling of his.

***

True isolation is to be surrounded by people in whom one dare not confide.

Jeremy's natural confidantes were Quentin and Hermione but, morally and intellectually, he was at odds with them. He was at odds with his parents. He was out-of-step with his former schoolfriends.

He had so looked forward to the reunion, convinced that it would offer an opportunity to air his anxieties. As so often in his teens, all hope now seemed to rest in Charlie Wimpole.

Progress Report.

The Deputy Vice-Chancellor's office was so different with Sir William as occupant than it had been under Sir Edward. Whilst many of the furnishings were the same, their re-arrangement removed the austerity, replacing it with a reassuring softness of line. Graft had become grace.

Quentin was welcomed warmly, offered a comfortable chair and the choice of tea, coffee, or a cold drink. Sir William disregarded the papers that lay before him and made small talk, with which he seemed at ease. Whilst, no doubt, this was one of the many facets that had secured him the post, there appeared to be nothing tokenistic about his inconsequential chatter.

Eventually, however, he riffled through the sheaf of papers, which he had clearly read beforehand, as he needed to refer to their detail only occasionally. "You seem to be confident that some definitive equations will be established within the next couple of months, Quentin." (He had never used 'Tinniswood' as a form of address.) "Good work. This is a most encouraging interim report, which will see me smoothly through my meeting with the Home Secretary. Thanks for that!" This final phrase was accompanied by the wry smile and crows' feet creases of habitual good humour. "Well done, also, upon securing young Mr. Chan's official involvement. I hope you agree that the project has reached the point beyond which it would have been unwise to proceed without Jeremy being fully signed-up."

"Yes, I do agree. That is a point that we need to discuss, though. It transpires that he has qualms."

"How has this manifested itself? Stroppy opposition? Loss of enthusiasm? A young man's sulks?"

"Silence."

"Silence? You mean he continues to work but has abandoned his conviviality? I can see that such behaviour would lead to a less comfortable atmosphere in the lab. but does it carry with it anything of greater consequence, do you think?"

"It's the kind of silence that is shouting all-day-long. Does that make sense?"

"Indeed it does. Have you approached him about his qualms?"

"Alas, I fear that's not my forte. I'm a Chemist, not a Counsellor!"

"Of course. And a brilliant Chemist, too! It would be both foolish and unfair of me to burden you further." Sir William was not of the old, militaristic school of management: *See to it, Sarn't Major*! whether the task be greasing guns or changing nappies. "What about Hermione? Might she be able to neutralise this unanticipated impediment to smooth progress?" Emollient to a fault, Sir William had been recruited neither from Industry nor from Politics; he was a career-serving product of the Foreign Office, whose Permanent Secretary he may well have become, had this particular opportunity not presented itself.

"She is certainly better-suited to the attempt than I!"

"Then may I ask you to task her? Please reassure her that she has my total backing, both in considering her the appropriate person for the job and as additional enforcer, should need arise."

He had paused (not stumbled) over the word 'enforcer'. This had been prompted, not by doubt nor by distaste, but by a calculated desire to reassure Quentin. It conveyed the effortless authority Sir William had intended. He paused for a few seconds, tidied the sheaf of papers, slipping them neatly into their manila folder, gave Quentin an almost cherubic smile, and thanked him for both his work and his time. "Come back to me at any time you feel the need but, if not before, may we meet in a month?"

Quentin left the office feeling much more at ease than he had entered it. Hermione, he knew, would willingly attempt to charm Jeremy back into the fold. Meanwhile, he could focus his mind upon Chemistry. He had Sir William's blessing.

Back To School (ii).

"Of course, you've been on my mind for a while, now." Charlie Wimpole was sitting in his 'I'm here to help' chair; Jeremy had automatically gravitated towards the 'let's get this sorted' corner of a two-seater settee. Old habits. They were in Charlie's small, neat, comfortable Sitting Room. The Housemaster's quarters were substantial and, thus, offered settings suitable for all occasions. The Study was strictly for business: admin., reprimands, difficult interviews, even the occasional inquisition. The Dining Room required gatherings of greater scale to fill its considerable dimensions: formal meals, drinks parties, the reception of minor dignitaries. Most Wimpoleites had an acquaintance with both of these rooms but few had entered the Sitting Room, which Charlie protected as 'his' space. However, he had always allowed its bastions to be stormed by trauma. Death, divorce, despair: each of these had found its way into the room, over the years. Jeremy, himself, had visited it on the occasion of his A Level choice family farrago. Thus he knew, instinctively, where to sit when Charlie had said, "Do make yourself comfortable in the Sitting Room, whilst I fix some drinks. What will you have?"

'Cheers' were exchanged. A while was spent on the success of the previous day. Additional snippets of information about Jeremy's peers were shared. Then there was a reflective silence. Jeremy looked out of the window. It offered a wonderful view across the grounds. Lush grass and mature trees were interspersed with formal flower beds, themselves packed with mid-summer colour. A few pupils, dressed in Sunday mufti, strolled, or sat, or lounged. There must have been a few in the cricket nets, just out of view but resonating a regular bat-on-ball thud and crack. It was not an awkward silence at all; quite comfortable, in fact. Comfortable and comforting. But, of course, it was a prelude. The direction of their conversation, once it resumed, was predictable; it was merely a matter of deciding which of the two would or should begin. Drawing upon his extensive experience of this scenario, Charlie adjudged it time to speak.

"Of course, you've been on my mind for a while, now. Did you know that I had received an unusual letter from the Deputy Vice-Chancellor's Office, regarding your reliability?"

"When?" Jeremy's response not only answered Charlie's question but its tone made him realise that he had unintentionally shocked the person who, more than anything else, he was seeking to reassure.

"No matter how many years I've done this job, I *still* get things wrong," he remonstrated with himself. As this was running through his mind, he said aloud, "Ah, so the answer's no. I'm sorry; I assumed you knew. Let me start again." And he explained how he had received the letter, taken the view that his response would be helpful to Jeremy, having been given the go-ahead by the Headmaster, and then slotted it into his mental 'pending' file. Only since he had viewed the list of those due to attend the reunion had his memory been stirred. The request seemed no more routine, several months later, than it had at the time and, thus, Jeremy's well-being *had* been on his mind. This is why, yesterday, he had suggested a chat.

Jeremy absorbed all of this attentively. He did not feel that Charlie had behaved inappropriately but he was intrigued that the request had come from the Deputy Vice-Chancellor, not from Quentin Tinniswood. He had never associated the two. That he needed advice became more urgently obvious to him. That Charlie would do his best to guide him, if asked, he did not doubt. But he had signed The Official Secrets' Act. What, *precisely*, was he permitted to reveal within the terms of that document? He had no idea.

Ordinarily, Charlie's clarification would have prompted Jeremy to outline his concerns. But there was nothing ordinary about his current position. News that the Deputy Vice-Chancellor was taking a surreptitious interest did nothing to alleviate his concerns. He maintained his silence.

"I'm sorry, ...", Charlie began but Jeremy's interruption sliced through the nascent sentence.

"There's no need to be. You've done nothing that merits apology." The words were intended to be emollient; their curt tone and rhythm made them sound acidic. More the product of resentful victimhood than of gratitude.

Charlie realised that he had unintentionally strayed over a border. He wondered whether he would be able to re-trace his path. Jeremy was no longer a boy; no longer his responsibility; no longer answerable to him. To heave-down the doors of Jeremy's resistance would be to exhibit the sensitivity of a bull elephant in musk. An idiom that would have raised an appreciative chuckle in class. But this was not class. Not territory in which he felt in control. He elected to let Jeremy make the next move. No matter how long it took.

"I had no idea that the Deputy Vice-Chancellor was involved," Jeremy ventured, eventually. "I'm in deeper than I realised."

Charlie was grateful for the code: 'I need your guidance but I'm constrained' is what was meant.

"This has always been a CTV-free zone," Charlie noted and could not stop himself from an habitual rider of self-mockery: "If it hasn't been, yours truly is comprehensively buggered!" This might have been considered ill-judged badinage. It turned-out to be welcome relief.

Jeremy visibly relaxed. Matching Charlie's exhibition of 'English wry', he looked him in the eyes and asked, in a melange of deadly seriousness and impish mischief, "What *is* the punishment for forcing someone into breaking The Official Secrets' Act?"

De-Brief.

Sunday brunch was a decidedly subdued affair. It had turned out to be a very late night and they had not stinted themselves. Once the plates had been cleared and quick coffees had been swallowed, they had returned to the bar, where they had remained for several hours. Jeremy did not linger. Having dispatched a restorative plate of Full English and multiple cups of tea, he began to excuse himself. He explained that he had promised Charlie W. a visit before he needed to catch his train back to Cambridge. "Great to catch-up, boys." he said, "Let's not leave it so long until next time." He paid his portion of the bill, picked-up his small overnight case, and disappeared through the door, in order to meet the taxi he had ordered.

Tom and Harry, somewhat revived by the excellent home-made sausages, decided to relax into a day-sustaining blow-out. More toast was ordered. "What did you make of him, then?" Tom asked, as they waited. "Even you noted the anti-capitalist stance. Do you think this Cuban bint's turned him into a Red Flag waver?" That the dreamy book-reader had made the transformation into sharp City slicker was not all that surprising. Although always fundamentally amiable, Tom had also always shown a sharper side.

"She doesn't live with him, anymore," Harry responded. "He was always on the pink side, remember. Always keen to separate himself from the crowd; that's why he played Goalie." Harry was lazy, in an attractive kind of way. He didn't like there to be 'issues'. He felt more confident viewing the world within the context of team sports – his natural comfort zone.

"He was on edge.   Didn't you notice that cold chip preoccupation?"

"Cold chip preoccupation? What are you on about?"

"Pushing a cold chip around and around his plate. In a world of his own. Not paying a blind bit of notice."

"Well, you know Jezza: the Day Room Philosopher!"

"Harry: get real! He's in some sort of trouble. Why else do you think he's carted-off to Charlie W.'s?"

Harry could not find a sufficiently escapist response.   Tom's pertinence had left him with no verbal duvet to snuggle under. Unhappily, he accepted that Tom was right. "But what can *we* do about it? If we don't know what's what?"   Ever-evasive, Harry began to feel a need to return to Yorkshire and to chatting-up potential clients for the sprawling acres he was tasked to sell. Complications quite sufficient for him, he felt.

"He's our mate, Harry. This is no time to bottle it. I'm going to give him a bell in a couple of days. If knowing what's what is necessary, I'll root it out and let you know!" Whilst he was inclined to be a bit pushy (a trait that served him well at work) Tom also had a more caring quality of character. It had been this that had made him the first amongst their peers to invite a young Malaysian to spend half-term with his family. It had been a huge success, subsequently copied by others, but shared, predominantly, between his and Harry's families. He might well be marble cold on the Trading Floor but he had his mellower moments.

Harry felt a little inadequate. He had had a lifetime of practising how to handle this. "Good man - be sure to let me know!"

It was time for them to take their separate ways but both knew that it would not be too long before they would be re-grouping.

How Best To Respond?

Whilst his letter had been addressed to both parents, the envelope bore his mother's name, alone. Suspicious of his father's pride, Jeremy had wanted to ensure that the letter was, at least, read by both, even if subsequently ignored. He had calculated that it was more likely than not that Geraldine would receive the post in which it would arrive and that, in the other event, the typed, British stamped envelope would arouse intrigue, rather than a determination to destroy. His father was, without doubt, difficult and demanding but he was not devious.

Receipt involved no complications. Geraldine was at home when the post arrived; Gerald was at the factory. She opened it, read it, relished it. Then she put it away in a secret place, the haunt of cherished treasures.

Whilst she was delighted that Jeremy had both made contact and indicated a wish to reconcile, she was equally aware that this was her only opportunity. Were she to fail to persuade Gerald that they *must* be encouraging in their reply, she knew that she would not be given a second chance. She was going to have to play this hand like a poker-player who knows that the held cards will be either fortune-making or ruinous.

Were she to respond to the excitement she felt, she would phone Gerald immediately. She was a wiser, a more patient woman than that. She was content to feel better by having read the letter than months of Dr. Woo's medication had made her feel. The pills, in combination with her secret knowledge, would now make her strong again. She would wait. She felt sure that she would know when to act. But she also knew how important it would be to Jeremy to know that she had received the letter and her response to it. *My dear, dear Jeremy*, she wrote within half-an-hour of reading what he had written, *I was so, so pleased to read your letter, today. I <u>know</u> your father will be equally delighted but I must ask you to exhibit patience. As you are aware, his ways are not well adapted to modern systems, modern outlooks. You must trust me to bide time; to await a propitious occasion; to ensure that he can do what I know to be in his heart but without loss of face. You must understand how, to <u>him</u>, this is so important, even if it makes no sense to you (or, indeed, to me.)* She took opportunity to bring her son up-to-date with all the family and local news – but she assiduously avoided mentioning her own impaired health.

***

Tom waited for a few days, wanting his call to seem natural, inconsequential. And then he dialled the number he had managed to extract from Jeremy at some point over the weekend. A few ring-tones triggered the voice-mail system. He did not want to leave a message, so he hung-up. This sequence was repeated several times during the evening. And the next. And the next. Tom decided that this would not do and, reluctantly, left a brief message, which he hoped would sound sufficiently insouciant not to arouse any suspicion: *Hi, Jezza. Tom, here. Great to catch-up over the weekend. I need to see a client in Cambridge, next week, any chance we can hook-up? Call me.* The Cambridge client was, of course, entirely fictitious but credible. His intention had been to talk over the phone: remoter, a bit more clinical. But he could not phrase a message that would bring this about without it blowing his cover. Jeremy, he knew, was quite capable of scenting subterfuge. This was Tom's clearer path.

***

"An interesting question!" Charlie Wimpole was responding to the point Jeremy had put to him about the punishment meted out to those who enforce a breaking of The Official Secrets' Act. "Are we talking Pub Quiz, here, or Public Prosecution?"

"Oh, most definitely the latter."

"Ouch!" A fortnight away from retiring, Charlie thought that he had faced pretty-well every vicissitude known to Man. Now, he knew he was wrong. "I don't have the faintest idea," he deflatedly confessed. A rare response. 'Charley W. knows everything' was a popular soubriquet that fed his daily vanity. "What price vanity when things *really* matter?" he pondered. "'Ask no questions and be told no lies' has always seemed defeatist all-round to me. It's not a million miles away from that other motto of mediocre morality: 'Don't ask; don't tell'. Were I to be asked I could, in all honesty, deny that I had pulled-out your finger nails, or water-boarded you! So: if you want to tell me your difficulty, I'm listening."

"It's more complicated than that. I feel the *need* to tell you but I'm not at all sure I *want* to. I know this sounds like semantic posturing; 'the one-time star of the Union firmament twinkles brilliantly before his ex-Housemaster. Shall we fence?' But it's not. I mean it. The distinction is crucial." He said no more.

"At the risk of sounding both petty and pompous, may I say that you are playing the part of the patient who visits his doctor, asking for medicine but refusing to explain the symptoms."

"Neither petty, nor pompous. Apt, if anything."

"O.K. So we seem to agree on everything apart from one small detail: how to proceed beyond this impasse. Your call!" Charlie's tone was one of frustration, rather than of impatience. An acknowledgement of impotence.

***

As he had anticipated, Hermione was quite willing to act on Quentin's behalf. She knew her husband's limitations and that the pressure on him of attempting to secure Jeremy's blessing re the SPA project would be counter-productive, all-round. She spent much of the weekend considering her task.

"He's bright, principled, more than a little naive, shocked," she reasoned. "Underlying all of this is *fear*. He's frightened to acknowledge that, already, he has contributed to the project. Frightened that he has been caught in a spider's web from which only a freak wind will release him. Frightened, perhaps more than anything, by the thought of the clinical trials. Of failure. It's not the possibility that his own work may fail – or falter – he doesn't have that kind of arrogance. It's the responsibility he would feel for any trialist whose entire memory might be erased, in error. That's the key." These thoughts helped to crystallise the strategy that was forming in her mind.

As they prepared for bed on Sunday night, she said to Quentin, "I know how I will approach him. I feel confident that I can win him over."

"I knew I could rely on you, m'dear. I hope all goes well." It was typical of him that he showed no curiosity. His intention had been to secure authorisation to divert responsibility to Hermione. That achieved, he considered it to be no longer his concern. A life-time of developing formulas that Industry might put to good or to ill had taught him not to dwell on matters beyond his immediate control. It was this capacity that had made Sir Edward Fitzmaurice select him, all those years ago.

***

She recognised the handwriting and was unsure whether to feel intrigued, irritated, or relieved. The envelope had been left c/o *The Politics (Postgraduates) Department.* Inside, was a neatly written note: *Dear Anita, Your course must be almost completed, by now, and I expect that it will not be long before you return home. Do you still regard Cuba as home? Or are you a little like me: home-less?!*

I'm attending a school reunion, this weekend. (Don't mock me!) I shall be back in Cambridge on Sunday evening. Coffee, for old times'sake. Sometime next week?

As ever,

Jeremy.

He was correct. Her dissertation had been completed some time since and she was merely awaiting the call for a *viva voce* to finalise the course. Her ticket back to Cuba had been booked for her by her government's education authorities. Of her three possible reactions to Jeremy's note, intrigue asserted itself. She circled his final sentence and proposed a day, time, and place, rather like a marginalised comment on an essay. She returned the note to its original envelope, scored-out her name and internal address, replacing it with Jeremy's, and dropped it into the Chemical Engineering Department, as she was passing.

***

He was holding an open return ticket. Whilst his arrival at Liverpool Street was later than he had intended, there was one more Cambridge-bound train to catch. He settled into a seat in an almost empty carriage. A late night, considerable indulgence, and emotional tension had exhausted him. He slept throughout the journey and had to be gently shaken awake, as his train pulled into its destination.

As he walked home, he reflected. There was much to reflect upon.

Checking his pigeon hole, he looked at the re-addressed envelope and felt slightly queasy. Part of him had anticipated that Anita would ignore his note, altogether. Part of him, even, had hoped that she would. Her response added a further complication to his life, at a time it yearned for simplicity. Then there was Tom's message, released by pressing the insistently-winking red button on his phone-set.

Might there be an obvious and rather neat tactic staring him in the face?

As he had calculated, Tom's cell-phone was busy and he was directed to voice-mail. This suited his purpose, which was practical rather than social. He repeated the day, time, and place proposed by Anita and hoped that Tom would be able to make it.

***

Hermione had swung into action on Monday morning. She felt that a confident performance had been received less than whole-heartedly by her audience. However, she was certain that she had made enough telling points for him to think about and to revise his stance, over the next few days. She countered Quentin's anxiety and encouragement to go back and try again with the argument that this would be too crude. Jeremy was both sensitive and intelligent; too heavy a hand was more likely to lose than to land him.

She had allowed him time to settle at his work station and only after a few hours had passed did she casually ask him how his reunion had been. This had enabled her to gauge how chatty (or not) he was feeling. Were she fly-fishing, it would have been a master class in technique. Patience and guile had been the hallmarks of her method. But, as yet, she was unable to present her catch.

Jeremy had never exhibited any interest in Field Sports. Not even to oppose them. Until now, they had been something he had simply never considered. Suddenly, his thoughts were directed towards the fox, the stag, the trout; the hare, the duck, the grouse, ... All manner of creatures pursued. Some to become food; some to become trophies. Detection, domination, and death: that was the common thread. These thoughts of Jeremy's were not pathetic, however. He was not identifying a shared victimhood. "Why," he asked himself, "is *so* much time, money, and effort spent in the pursuit of these beasts?" It did not take him long to reach a conclusion: "Because they make themselves difficult to bag. They do everything they can to evade capture. They are 'sport'. Their pursuers celebrate them; revere them for it." He became preternaturally calm, incisive: "I'll give them a run for their money!" he determined.

***

For one brief, extra-mischievous moment, Jeremy had considered not appearing at the designated cafe. He had envisaged Anita and Tom, sitting alone at separate tables and wondering why he had not shown up. He had even projected the imagined scene into their exchanging frustrations about people who failed to keep appointments. Of joining over another coffee and of discovering that they had an absentee friend in common.

Tempting though this had been, Jeremy lacked the necessary malice. He would be true to his word. He always was.

As expected, the cafe was crowded. Of the three, Jeremy was the first to arrive. His father being a strict time-keeper, combined with the regime of bells and time-tables at school had made him somewhat time-obsessed. He ordered his drink, selected a table large enough for three, settled, and speculated upon who might appear first. In all likelihood, it would be Tom, another member of the 'summoned by bells' brotherhood. Anita's time-keeping was quintessentially Latin. As he waited, he wondered why either of them had proposed a meeting, let alone both of them in the same week. 'That way lies paranoia', an inner voice warned him. It had been *he* who had sent the note to Anita, half-hearted though it had been in intention. Similarly, *he* had told both Harry and Tom that they should keep in closer contact, in future. If Tom had to come to Cambridge, anyway, he was guilty of nothing more sinister than agreement. *If* - but the warning inner-voice spoke again, rebuking him for excessive suspicion. He began to feel guilty that he had set-up this ruse. It had been somewhat ignoble of him.

It is said that truth can be stranger than fiction. This was the maxim that burst into Jeremy's mind, prompted by what he saw happening at the cafe's entrance. Two people had arrived at the door simultaneously; a man and a woman. The former had held the door for the latter with exaggerated comic gallantry, followed by spontaneous and shared laughter. They were Tom and Anita!

Both spotted Jeremy, waved, and made towards his table. Only upon arrival did they fully understand that theirs was a shared destination. Their former relaxed, casual ease acquired a sudden tension. They exchanged slightly bewildered looks and hovered behind empty chairs, unsure whether or not to sit in them. Jeremy, meanwhile, had attempted a masquerade of unruffled charm. "Name your poison; my treat," he proffered, rising and ready to head to the service counter.

"Double espresso, please," Anita requested, her tone as neutral as she could make it.

"I'll have cappuccino, please Jezza, - chocolate on top." The rider came as he pulled back a chair for Anita and helped her to settle. Tom's auto-charm had kicked-in. Someone less adept may have then taken his own seat and shared an agonising silence, waiting for their host to return with the coffees. Not so, Tom. He initiated an exchange of names and masterfully controlled any sense of recognising hers as belonging to "that Cuban bint", as he had called her, only a few days before. "Another Chemical Engineer?" he disingenuously enquired. "Oh, Politics - much more my thing!" Skilfully, he insinuated himself into an exchange of pleasantries. Had he been auditioning for the part of Satan in Eden, it would have required a potent performance to steal the part from him. Jeremy's return with the coffees brought his blandishments to a timely conclusion.

"I hope you don't mind," Jeremy opened, as he resumed his seat. "I don't get out of the lab. on weekdays very often, so I went for a combo." Inwardly, he was feeling quite embarrassed but he made a good fist of presenting this as a perfectly normal arrangement. There was even the implied suggestion that if either of them felt otherwise, theirs was the peculiarity.

Anita had assumed that this meeting would offer an opportunity for her and Jeremy to tidy-up some pretty ragged loose-ends. Tom had his own agenda. Pleasant enough though the cafe encounter became, neither achieved their objective. Eventually, passing time and growing realisation combined to conclude the occasion. Tom needed to pursue his client-meeting fiction; Jeremy was expected back at the lab.; Anita had her *viva voce* to prepare.

In For A Penny ... .

Once again, Charlie Wimpole found himself refereeing two opposing inclinations: to leave well alone/to act.

In moments of self-reflection he acknowledged a fundamental flaw in his character. It was a form of arrogance; it had never, thus far, proved fatal but it had brought him, at times, dangerously close to the wind. He could no longer kid himself that he didn't recognise its potential for damage than could smokers kid themselves that they were ignorant of the self-destruction they were involved in. Yet, like them, he persisted.

"I can resolve this," was Charlie's weakness. Worse: "I *will* resolve this"!

His meeting with Jeremy, the day after the reunion, had consisted more of silence than of discussion. Details of 'the family upset' had been clarified; also, the end of his affair with Anita. But nothing more than its enigmatic mention had evolved, regarding The Official Secrets' Act. With respect to this issue Jeremy's obduracy had been entire. He *would not* say more.

Charlie found himself in that most impenetrable of forests: knowing more than he found to be comfortable and less than he needed to be able to establish any bearings.

It was a rash decision but he was resolute.

Dear Deputy Vice-Chancellor,

You may recall that you wrote to me a short while ago, requesting a character reference on a former pupil of this school towards whom I held a position of especial responsibility.

Recourse to the relevant file will re-acquaint you with my response. It was brief and business-like. Some might say terse. A range of factors may explain this: the context of your request made it peculiar; I felt under constraint, as an employee; I was anxious to do all I could to support a former member of my House whom I regard highly, whilst seeking to avoid unnecessary incursion. As may have been apparent upon receipt, it was not a letter with which I felt entirely at ease. My estimation of Jeremy Chan's character remains as it was; my concern over why it should have been sought in the first place is much increased.

Recently, I have become aware that Jeremy feels under particular pressure. He has split with a former girlfriend and there have been disagreeable exchanges with his parents. Neither of these misfortunes may account for his current state of mind. He is articulate about them both; his work at Cambridge, however, appears to carry the 'avoid at all costs' signals of a Government Health Warning. I have done this job for too long not to be confident that there is something amiss and not to know that the nucleus of the problem relates directly to the request you made of me, a few months ago.

Thus, I feel morally obliged to press you for details. In doing so, may I stress that I am writing personally, and not as an emissary of the school, from which I am due to retire at the end of this term. Put crudely, Sir, were you inclined to cite my employment prospects as cause for withdrawal, such a route would prove to be a cul du sac!

I am afraid that you will find this letter to be distasteful, possibly disrespectful. To me, that is cause for regret. It is, however, a letter which I may not shrink from writing.

To ignore me and to decline a response would be unfortunate. No doubt you will note that I am resolved to support my former charge, regardless of any inconvenience in doing so that may arise.

I look forward to your earliest response.

Yours sincerely,

Charles Wimpole.

In his early days and with mechanical type-writer and carbon paper, his first draft would be the one to be sent. However, now that he had exchanged his trusty portable for a lap-top and graduated to word-processing, Charlie was able to read, re-read, trim, tamper, and edit at will. Eventually, he felt satisfied that he had written as judiciously as the situation allowed. He deliberately elected not to copy-in his Headmaster. This was, in his view, a solo-mission. That it was likely to be met mildly was not his expectation. The two sheets of A4 were folded crisply, slotted into an envelope, which was neatly addressed and headed 'Personal'. Eschewing the school's postal system, he took it to a letter box in town, from which he knew he would not be able to withdraw it, later. The blue touch-paper had been lit; he stood back to note the inevitable explosion.

***

If an arrogant belief in his ability to make a difference was one facet of Charlie Wimpole's default position, pernicketiness and a compulsive attention to the most minute detail was another. Thus, he had diligently copied his letter twice: one for Jeremy's file, which (along with many others) remained intact and one for his former pupil, sent as an email attachment and accompanied by a brief message:

Dear Jeremy,

I appreciated and respected your decision to visit me on Sunday and for reasons greatly in excess of retirement goodwill! That it was possible for us to consider family and girlfriend misalliance returned us to where we knew each other best. But there was something of far greater moment that eluded us. Forgive me; I'm both interfering and infuriating but, to be a little bit camp, 'A Housemaster's Not Just For Christmas'! (I can't believe I've just written that!)

Curse me if it helps but the die is cast. Letter to D V-C attached.

Charlie W.

***

Then began the preparations for his retirement. Meticulous by nature, Charlie had little to do other than to start packing himself up, ready to move. There was a bit of topping and tailing and of double-checking the paperwork was in order. He had a few sessions with his elected successor. And there were a number of parties. He loved a party! During the interludes, he began to doubt his action. There had been scrapes and near-squeaks, before, but nothing quite like this. Was he, he wondered,

deliberately creating a crisis to fill the ensuing vacuum? NO!
He could honestly deny that self-accusation. This was not of his
making. But it *did* demand his attention. About that he was
convinced.

There would be ugliness. This, also, he accepted. Step on the
toes of the establishment and it knows but one method of
response: straight to the top. Pointless though it would be,
remonstration would follow. It would be couched more in
sadness than in anger. There would be regrets that so late a
blemish should be sustained. Depending upon the degree of
outrage expressed, there may even be an opportunity taken to
focus upon issues previously side-stepped. It couldn't be helped.
The letter had been posted; the copy had been sent.

Reflections & Connections.

"May I take a couple of weeks off?"

Neither Quentin nor Hermione knew quite how to react. Jeremy was almost half-way through the standard PhD three years. He had worked tirelessly. The couple of hours he had taken in order to meet Tom and Anita for coffee had been his only time-off from lab. hours, so far. That his own research was of Doctoral potential was not in doubt. His contribution to the progress of SPA could not be contested. Quentin had no qualms about his next regular monthly meeting with the Deputy Vice-Chancellor. To reject Jeremy's request would be to exercise both unreasonable and uncharacteristic inflexibility. It would also destroy their weeks of careful nurturing.

A respectable pause was followed by Quentin's question, "Do you have anywhere in mind?"

"No, I'm not going anywhere. I just fancy a bit of space. I've plenty of writing-up to get on with." Jeremy had practised lightness of touch.

"Request granted!" declared Quentin, deliberately mocking his professorial elevation.

"Should we say starting on Monday?" Again, he managed to make it sound as if he were not too bothered which Monday was in question. His deceitful deftness of touch had, initially, shocked him. Subsequently, he had come to disregard it.

***

I've passed my viva voce. It's Anita del Azura, MPhil (Cantab), from now on! Is there any chance of our having dinner before I go home? (Preferably without Tom, utterly charming though he is!)

***

Charlie,

I've got a couple of weeks off. We should meet. (Yes, I am a tad pissed-off but also yes, I know you mean well.) Suggest a time.

J.

***

Mr. Jeremy Chan*:*

It was an invitation from the Deputy Vice-Chancellor, printed on stiff card and in bold, raised copperplate. At the bottom right corner was a hand-written *P.T.O.* Overleaf, and again in handwriting, was the following note: *We have never met. My omission. I wonder if you might care to be one of my personal guests at this forthcoming formal dinner. Were you to find this agreeable, I am minded to invite your former Housemaster, Charles Wimpole, also.*

Best,

William Abercrombie.

***

Having received his mother's most recent letter, craving patience, Jeremy had sent a text to say *All cool, Mom. Keep in touch.* He was as anxious as she to hold tight to the hope of reconciliation.

***

He did not know why but he felt an urgent need to put his personal house in order. He wanted all the ragged hems of his personal relationships to be trimmed or turned-up. This is why he had sent his mother the text. He planned to meet Charlie Wimpole as soon as he could (and he had already sent him a clinical email, concerning the Abercrombie Dinner: *No idea what's behind this but I think we should both accept.*) Without doubt, he should meet-up with Anita and, to that end, he replied to her immediately, congratulating her upon her degree and suggesting a sequence of evenings for her to choose from.

***

It was as if he were setting-out to ensure all his bases were covered. The kind of approach, in a young man, associated with terminal illness. When this thought entered his mind, he dismissed it as being melodramatic. The truth was that he sought the untrammelled freedom of a wild creature. He was paring himself to minimal bulk, in anticipation of responses that may require him to be fleet of foot.

Come, Dine With Me.

"I've had time, since my MPhil. was confirmed, to set about sorting through what I'm going to take back with me to Cuba and what I'm going to discard." Anita and Jeremy had agreed to dine on neutral ground. The restaurant they had selected was new to both of them and, thus, carried with it no memories for either. "Material items have proved to be fairly easy - what is the point of a winter-weight overcoat in Cuba, no matter how *fashionista* a statement it may be? It's the ephemera that I've had difficulties with. Not excess baggage issues, admittedly, but I still feel the need to sift and to sort." She was far from feisty, this evening. Less emotionally carmine clad and more the bereaved widow, dressed in relentless black. "I've spent the last two years of my life at one of the most elite establishments in the world. My teachers, my lodgings, my social acquaintances, all defined by 'privilege' – true, even the most impoverished full-scholarship undergraduate to be found in the entire university. Within a few days, I shall be back in Havana; oh and I know, before you say it, that I shall still be privileged but it will take time to re-adjust." She twirled a bread stick in her wine glass, pensively.

The focus of her conversation caused Jeremy, also, to contrast where they were with where he had come from. Another place of privilege but also far away, both in miles and in manner. It also made him contrast his position with Anita's. She would shortly return home to be reunited with climate, family, culture; he felt marooned - a cultural castaway!

***

Even though London was an easy train journey from Cambridge, Jeremy's work and life-style habits had seen him rarely taking the trip. As a convenient, mid-way, meeting place it served his and Charlie Wimpole's purposes well. They met in a pub immediately opposite the selected restaurant. Charlie was extremely anxious to crave Jeremy's forgiveness for what may have been considered a form of moral colonialism: striking a pose with the Deputy Vice-Chancellor on his behalf but not at his behest. An awkward moment but quickly passed.

They crossed the road and settled at their table. Deciding that they would have much to discuss, they concentrated on the menu and placed their orders. Once the wine had been presented, there was nothing to impede their conversation. Unlike the previous occasion upon which they had met, silence seemed to have been excluded. They were like colts turned out of stables and into grass, at the end of winter. So carefree did Jeremy seem to be that Charlie concluded that the millstone, whatever it may have been, had been cut free. Certainly, he was very up-beat about 'home issues'. That he and Geraldine were back in touch (no matter how slight) was evidently cause for huge relief. There was clear optimism that it would be merely a matter of time before he and Gerald found a way to re-connect. Details of the dinner with Anita were also full of sunlight. Their friendship had been restored and neither felt bitter to have lost their closer relationship, which both had agreed would probably not have survived her return to Cuba, in any case.

All of this occupied both starters and the main course. Not until the sweet trolley had been wheeled away was their next dinner alluded to. Anxious not to compound his intrusiveness, Charlie had assiduously avoided the topic. It was Jeremy who launched into it. "So, Charlie, we are to dine at the Deputy Vice-Chancellor's table!" His tone was surprising. It was neither mordant nor cynical but enthusiastic, even excited.

"Indeed we are, young Chan!" Charlie sustained the rally with equal levity of inflexion. "Could this be the prelude to the higher calling of Birthday Honours, mayhap?!"

Shared laughter. Shared delight. "But is this real?" Charlie wondered, as he followed where his former pupil led. He still had no idea what had weighed so heavily, a couple of weeks before. Why he had asked that question about The Official Secrets' Act still nagged at the elder man's consciousness.

"Have you any idea what kind of a do it will be?" Charlie asked.

"Not the faintest. Full-fig, obviously, given the 'Black Tie' dress code edict. Probably a College Feast. Sherry to be sipped judiciously in the D V-C's commodious quarters, prior to processing t'wards our dining destination!" Jeremy revelled in a grotesque *basso-profundo*, coloured by a studiously arcane style of delivery.

"Accompanied, *sans doute*, by a faithful College retainer, possessed of little neck, a stubby nose, and a bowler hat!" Charlie matched him, absurdity for absurdity.

"Caparisoned in silken stockings, knickerbockers, frock coat, and silver-buckled patent leather footwear, whilst carrying a ceremonial mace, the orb of which has been dutifully polished by members of this same family since the sixteenth century!"

What a contrast this was with their previous interchange of silences.

Evidently, it was not to be a College Feast, nor even a large gathering. The Deputy Vice-Chancellor's office had been transformed into an intimate dining space. In the centre was an elegant table, surrounded by eight chairs with place-settings before each. Joining instructions had followed the original invitation. Guests were respectfully asked to arrive promptly. There were to be no pre-prandials; a direct move to table would be executed. That having been said, this was to be no simple supper. The battery of glasses and the armoury of cutlery surrounding each place-setting indicated that Sir William intended it to be quite a campaign.

The guests, obedient to their host's bidding, were assembled and invited to table. Sir William stood at its head, signalling the others to sit, as directed. Commanding the foot of the table was the Home Secretary, flanked to right and to left by Quentin Tinniswood and Hermione Carstairs. Occupying the central area were the Heads of MI5 and MI6. As Sir William's personal guests, Jeremy and Charlie sat to his right and to his left. Still standing, his commanding presence drew their attention. "Ladies and Gentlemen, welcome. Following dinner, Professor Tinniswood will offer a short presentation; meanwhile, may I hope that you enjoy wine, food, and each other's company." He then took his seat. It had not been a Grace, nor had it been a Toast, but it had certainly made its mark. Jeremy immediately noted that there were five men and three women; he wondered whether a sudden decision to invite himself and Charlie had resulted in this slight imbalance. Given the identity of the other guests, he also wondered why on earth he and Charlie had been summoned, at all!

Much Improved.

Geraldine's health improved, dramatically. Her appetite returned; she slept soundly and without disturbance; the dreadful drenchings of uncontrollable sweat ceased. Her recently acquired habits of drawing the curtains, in order to shut the world out of her life, and of needing (literally) to talk herself into being able to leave the house, when leaving it was absolutely necessary, were replaced by her more customary relish of everything the world had to offer her. Those terrible journeys to the supermarket, where she would ponderously and indecisively parade the aisles, sometimes returning to the shelves from her basket far more than she finally took to the check-out, reverted to sprightly and inventive shopping expeditions. This resulted in the evening meal she shared with Gerald being restored to the occasion of taste and talk it had once been before a pall had extinguished its sparkle.

An undemonstrative man, Gerald made no comment about his wife's return to what Fothergill may have called "good form". But he was both aware of it and delighted by it. Whilst Geraldine yearned to raise the topic of Jeremy's letter and subsequent text, she had decided to wait for a lead from Gerald. She had assumed that her renewed spirits would prompt a comment which, in turn, would smoothly elide into the subject so close to her heart. On several occasions, she thought the moment had arrived. Enthusiastic compliments about the cooking; appreciative comments about the floral displays which she had returned to creating; agreements with social suggestions she had once again started to make. There had never been an allusion to her rediscovered well-being, however.

Eventually, she recognised that her policy of patience was flawed. She must decide whether to leave matters as they were, privately comforted by her knowledge that they and their son were no longer estranged, even if they remained distanced, or to take the initiative, herself. She plumped for the latter.

Although it was months before Chinese New Year, early booking lowered air fares. As a conversation about going to visit friends in Singapore petered-out, Geraldine took the opportunity to wonder how long it had been since they had last celebrated New Year in London, rather than their usual trip to New York. She knew the precise answer but it was the only line she felt able to take, tangential though it may be. Surprisingly, Gerald appeared happy to pursue not only the question but its implied suggestion: that they plan to visit the UK, next February. Booking now, he agreed, would secure a beneficial discount. His alacrity was such that Geraldine's true target was missed. She had anticipated some need for persuasion which, itself, may offer an opportunity to lure into their exchange the unofficially banned subject of their son. In this, she had been thwarted. However, by securing Gerald's agreement to the trip, thousands of miles distance between them and Jeremy would be reduced to tens. It may be slow but it was, she felt, progress. Ever the diplomat, she decided that she should settle for this arrangement, without attempting to force the issue further.

Musical Chairs.

It was a memorable meal. Course after course of small but delicious portions appeared, accompanied by an array of perfectly matched wines. Sir William made both Charlie and Jeremy feel welcome with his urbane conversation, appropriately spiced with anecdotes bordering upon but never transgressing into the *risqué*. He was adept, also, at inviting them to contribute. The table was small and intimate enough for him to be in touch with the other diners. This, especially, ensured that the two Intelligence Service Heads did not feel marooned in its middle reaches. (Returning to his earlier observation, Jeremy assumed that it had been originally intended that they would occupy the seats now taken by himself and Charlie.)

Each diner had an individual menu, beautifully printed on a small card, for consultation and as a memento. It proposed a sorbet after the main course, then a pudding, followed by a savoury &/or cheese. "Not exactly conventional in its approach," Sir William noted, have tinkled a tiny silver bell, as the main course plates were being cleared, and risen to offer "... a short directive!" "Not exactly conventional in its approach but, may I suggest, the breaking of convention, be it social, administrative, or, indeed, moral is that engine which we call progress!" He went on to outline a slight re-adjustment in the seating arrangements for these final courses. Charlie was invited to exchange places with Quentin, placing him to the Home Secretary's right and giving Quentin the opportunity, if necessary, to finalise with Sir William the details of his forthcoming presentation. Jeremy was re-positioned into a triangle that placed him between Hermione and the Head of MI5, with the Head of MI6 immediately opposite.

Whilst she did not ignore Hermione, with whom she had been chatting for much of the earlier phase of the dinner, the Home Secretary directed much of her attention to Charlie. She had read English, as an undergraduate, before pursuing a Law Conversion course and then qualifying as a Barrister. Accordingly, her initial themes were literary. Unfazed by her political office, Charlie discovered that she responded well to his cocktail of charm, knowledge, and gentle teasing. They established a shared taste for Dickens, contemporary American fiction, and the Romantic poets. "I bet you didn't admit to that when you were interviewed for your current post!" Charlie tossed this into their chatter with a lightness of touch that could do nothing more harmful than trigger a momentary cascade of giggles.

"Yes, an appetite for anti-establishment writers may not be seen as the ideal platform for a Home Secretary to pontificate from   - platform from which a Home Secretary might pontificate, perhaps I should say before I'm issued with a 'never end with a preposition' sanction!" A girlish delight in banter belied the onerous duties of her office. Then, as an afterthought, she added, maintaining the cut-and-thrust exchange, "Mind you, neither might it be considered the ideal platform for a Teacher – let alone a Housemaster!"

With the agility of a gazelle, she jinxed from literary tastes to his work-in-general and onto his specific sense of responsibility for his former charges after they had left school. It was a dazzling display, deploying the well-honed skills of the Barrister she once had been. It was constructed from an unexpected change of direction, of tone, of purpose, such as would render a witness slightly wrong-footed and would inject a jury with an almost electrical charge of urgency. Charlie found that he had no sufficiently tongue-in-cheek reply at his disposal to restore their previous display of light-hearted dexterity. Sincerity was his only available resource.

Hermione, meanwhile, ensured that Jeremy and the Head of MI6 were well acquainted. A well-travelled woman, she had visited Kuala Lumpur a number of times and, indeed, it transpired that she and Jeremy's family had acquaintances in common. Without ever feeling that he was being interviewed, let alone questioned, he did begin to realise that he had volunteered a considerable volume of information about himself, which she had the knack of effortlessly acquiring   -   like a winkle from its shell or a pomegranate seed from its pod.

Coffee and *petites fours,* accompanied by a choice of Port, Madeira, Cognac, or Malt Whiskey (Sir William's family had historical associations with Ireland) brought the dinner to a satiated conclusion. They also brought Sir William back to his feet. "I do hope that you have all enjoyed the past few hours at least as much as I have enjoyed them, myself. It has been a pleasure to act as your host. If I may ask you just to make minor adjustments in the direction of your chairs, you will all be able to see the screen onto which Professor Tinniswood will project various images designed to support his short presentation regarding a project that pertains to us all. Professor Tinniswood, I know, will not be offended if I withdraw, having been briefed, earlier, and might I ask Mr. Wimpole if he would care to join me in a nightcap? Quentin, do continue. Charlie, would you care to step this way?"

These simple words carried the patina of a Diplomat's long service. Flawlessly courteous, they were decisive and insistent. They were received without demur, acted upon without question. Chairs were slightly adjusted; Quentin moved to the projector, which had been activated, unobtrusively, by a steward, who then withdrew; Charlie Wimpole rose and moved in the direction of Sir William's gesture, bidding and receiving "Goodnight", as he left.

The Morning After ... .

Charlie knew that the dinner would end too late for him to return to school that night and he had, thus, secured a spare bed at Jeremy's flat. Out of habit, Jeremy had given him a key, even though he imagined that they would return from the dinner together. In the event, they did not coincide until the next morning.

"I didn't hear you come in," Charlie noted, "it must have been late. I didn't leave Sir William, myself, until gone 1.00."

"Yes, it was very late." Jeremy appeared to have retreated back into the almost autistic world he was occupying on the weekend of the reunion. "I'm *really sorry*, Charlie!" he suddenly burst out, expressing tremendous anger. "They had *no right*; I don't care who the hell they are. They dismissed you from that room as if you were a kid being sent away from an unsuitable T.V. programme. It was *so* insulting!"

"Sir William came with me to hold my hand; I wasn't sent all alone into the dark!" It was a characteristic of his when he was anxious to keep a potentially explosive issue under control: mock it; expose any absurdity it offered; distance it from personal involvement.

"NO! DON'T DO THAT! DON'T DENY THE INSULT!" And he left the room.

This was Jeremy's flat; Charlie was a mere visitor. If Jeremy wished to shout, he had every right to shout loud and clear; Charlie had *no* right to curtail him. That was his view, anyway.

***

As he had walked back from the dinner party, in the early hours of the morning, Charlie W. had reflected upon one of the strangest evenings of his life. Such a great deal of trouble had been taken to court him; for it to end as it had. It seemed to be strangely at odds. Sir William's patrician suavity had diminished not one jot, as they had made their way to a cosy little snug, further down the corridor that housed his office. He had continued to play the benevolent host, totally ignoring the course of action he had, himself, initiated. He had not apologised, not attempted to explain, not made the slightest reference to it, as he served a further generous measure of the very smooth Irish Malt. He and it were of the same mash. As each of them sipped, he had held forth on the increasing demands of high-office, wishing Charlie well with his forthcoming retirement and humorously berating himself for preaching to the converted. He had gone on to bemoan the lack of opportunity he had to entertain on a small scale. "Of course, Cambridge feeds at feasts! Vast numbers of guests, strange faces, visiting dignitaries. All too often, nowadays, potential benefactors to be groomed. And they're all very grand occasions that I would not consider trying to avoid. But an intimate dinner at which one can speak to and hear from all-at-table, ... a rare privilege. There again, of course, the more welcome when chance arises! I'm so glad that you could come." The final sentence had been effortlessly timed to perfection. Its close had coincided, precisely, with Charlie putting-down his empty glass. It was both as courteous and as definitive as had been the earlier masterstroke that had evicted him from Professor Tinniswood's presentation.

Of course, the streets he had walked along were far from deserted. A fair number of undergraduates were weaving their way from one just-closed pub to another, later-opening establishment. There was, however, that night-time ambience, ideally suited to reflection. For Jeremy to be closeted with the Home Secretary and both Heads of British Intelligence in a meeting from which he, himself, had been expressly excluded might be cause for admiration of his former pupil's kudos; it might, also, be cause for concern. The ghost of that question Jeremy had asked him about The Official Secrets' Act shimmied around a corner and chilled him, uncomfortably.

***

"I don't suppose we will see Jeremy, today," Quentin observed, as he placidly munched his toast. Even on a Saturday, all three of them normally went in for the morning; Quentin, himself, usually stayed all day. The fortnight's leave had been followed by a return to regular lab. attendance. Whilst it had been considered wiser to avoid pressure, Quentin and Hermione surmised that Jeremy had used the short holiday to survey his work and its incidental contribution to SPA. They had been mildly optimistic that their young assistant's doubts had diminished. He had returned noticeably lighter in mood. They had hoped that the dinner and the presentation would finalise matters.

"Will we see him, full-stop?" asked Hermione, more of herself than of Quentin, whom she knew to be a mostly silent breakfaster. Predictably, he continued to munch, to sip his tea, to glance at the scientific magazine he habitually read at this time of day. "He had seemed so relaxed during dinner, I honestly believed him to have become reconciled to the project. Still, it was quite an exhibition he offered us. One the Home Secretary won't forget in a long time!"

***

"Do you have to go straight back? Any chance of extending your ticket of leave until tomorrow?" Jeremy had returned to the small kitchen. Charlie had remained at the table, drinking his coffee in what he attempted to persuade himself was an unruffled manner. "I'm sorry I shouted but I think you know it was not really at you."

"You're upset. No, that's not right: you're angry. Angry people shout. May I make you some coffee?" He rose and made his way to the kettle, saying that he felt the circumstances merited his elongated absence from school. "One of the great advantages of Study Leave at exam-tide: hardly any pupils to teach! I'll phone to say I can't get back until tomorrow. The House is covered, this weekend, anyway."

Jeremy joined him at the table and sipped his coffee. "I'm going to abandon my PhD," he suddenly announced. "I'll need a job. Know of anywhere looking for an unqualified Chemistry teacher?"

Crisis Management.

Charlie spent his train journey going over and over his attempts to dissuade Jeremy from his determination. The more he re-ran the screenplay, the more he felt he could have marshalled no more lines of argument than he had. However, this did not reduce the frustration of his failure.

His final assault had been along the lines of: "How will abandoning your Doctorate help you to escape from whatever nightmare of officialdom you are in but cannot explain? As far as I can understand it, your issue concerns a possible outcome of your work which is already in train - just as you are already implicated. Whatever it is you're up against, surely the more authoritative your position the better."

Jeremy had refused to counter this. He had fallen back on that most irritating of defences that Charlie had heard so often from so many: "You don't understand!"

"Then let me. *Make* me understand."

"I can't."

"Can't or won't?"

"Charlie, let's not fall out. Drop it and go, before we do."

***

Quentin was shattered when he opened the letter. He had allowed himself to believe that Jeremy's display of anger at his presentation was probably fuelled by Sir William's lavish hospitality and that it was more a young man's melodrama than anything really serious. When he and Hermione had exchanged remarks at breakfast, the following morning, he had not given her comment due regard.

It was as much the letter's brevity and detached style that shook him as its content. *Dear Quentin,* it had opened. There was no attempt to adopt the pose of offended formality. No devices of any sort were employed to inject spleen in what followed. *I find myself unable to continue my postgraduate studies. I do not believe I have left anything of significance at the lab., thus there is no need for me to return. I enclose my keys.*

Regards to you and to Hermione.

Yours, Jeremy.

***

Dear Jeremy,

As you know, Quentin and I are a team. He has asked me to reply to your letter, which was addressed to him but signed-off to us both. He is a man of few words, be they spoken or written (outside of his books and articles.) Thus, whilst I am the author, the sentiment is shared.

We urge you to reconsider your decision to jettison your hard (and excellent) work of the past two years. Your findings, to date, are already worthy of a Doctorate, even though there is, technically, a year yet to go. Were you to write them up, Quentin would more than happily support their presentation to the awarding committee. Yours is a rare talent; to see it wasted would break Quentin's heart.

Of course, we understand what lies behind your decision. However, your dislike of one particular end to which your experiments have contributed should not overshadow the quite different ends to which they may also be put. Ends with which you would feel comfortable, even proud. It has been the scientist's curse, ever since Prometheus gave fire to mankind, to harness powers that may offer such essential benefits but which may also be put to mischief.

As you are aware, neither Quentin nor I feel that SPA, in the right hands, offends. We believe it to be a potential life-saver. Once it is known to exist, there will be no point in using torture to extract information; no need to indulge in state-sponsored murder. We truly believe it to be of human (and humane) benefice, as we have believed all of our 'special work', over the years, to be. I had hoped to have convinced you of this and I shall always hold myself responsible for failing to do so.

*Take as long as you want but think it through. We - **I** implore you.*

Our fondest best wishes,

Quentin & Hermione.

***

Sir William, of course, had not attended Quentin's post-dinner presentation. He had been busy, amputating Charlie from the gathering.   Thus, he had not witnessed Jeremy's outburst of moral incandescence.   But it had been reported to him.

"I understand that your protégée transmogrified himself, briefly, into a prisoner of conscience," he had observed when talking to Quentin the following week.   "Keep me informed, if you would." As always, Quentin was punctiliously obedient.   News of Jeremy's letter was duly conveyed.   This prompted an email from Sir William: *Q., Make an appointment soonest. W.*

Never exactly ruffled, the Deputy Vice-Chancellor showed some capacity for mild irritation.   "He's become a loose cannon, Quentin, and *this* Ship's Captain prefers his cannons firmly fixed. Attend to it, if you would."

"I am, ... I *was* his PhD supervisor, not his warden," Quentin's response began, in a register more akin to Hermione's impetuosity than to his own habitual phlegmatic detachment. The sentence was strangled before it could reach its end.

"That is disingenuous of you, Quentin! You *knew* your role was more than merely academic from the moment you were asked to take him on. From the moment you *agreed* to take him on!" The precise rephrasing of the observation was typical of Sir William's sensitivity to nuance. His view of the world and his expression of that view were calibrated with an exactness few others could (or would wish to) emulate. "Now, let us focus. Young Chan is displaying an unforeseen post-adolescent instability. His resolve needs to be stiffened. *You* must find the means to stiffen it!"

"I thought Hermione would be able to bring him back on board ..."

"But she didn't!" came the interjection. "When one route prevents access, what is the only sensible course of action to take? Seek another!"

"In all honesty, if *she* failed, it is irrational to think that *I* might succeed." Quentin was being more subtle than plain stubborn. His candour and reason were inescapable. Sir William was bound to recognise the fact.

"I agree. With due respect, your attempt would both fail and waste time. Thus, an alternative strategy is required. I shall contact that Housemaster of his."

There was a finality about the proposal that did not offer itself to Quentin for his opinion. Unworldly though he was, he could recognise a *fait accomplit* when one was presented to him. The emergency meeting was over.

In Touch.

Tom's miscued attempt to talk with Jeremy in Cambridge had irritated him. Fiercely competitive, he regarded his friend's finesse as a challenge. He would attempt to force Jeremy into an away fixture, thereby disadvantaging him. He decided upon a simple text-message: *omg, w/e plans aborted. Will b home-alone & bored. Any chance u cd join me?*

This had been sent and received part way through the fortnight Jeremy had taken off. What with catching-up with Anita, meeting Charlie in London, and needing to address a whole raft of minor matters that had escaped his attention for too long, he, genuinely, could not spare the time. He had replied: *soz, no way, this w/e. When free next?* Thus, eventually, arrangements had been fixed for him to stay the weekend with Tom, in London, aiming to arrive on Friday evening. The Friday which fell two weeks after Sir William's dinner.

Given his exchange with Charlie, his letter to Quentin and Hermione, the radical decision he had reached, and his recognition that, once he had finalised it, his funds would quickly dry-up, he toyed with cancelling his visit to Tom. But then Hermione's reply had arrived. Although he had a reputation for self-reliance, he was not so arrogant as to think that he could cope alone. On the other hand, having come so close to severing links with Charlie W., he wondered whether he dare risk an encounter with Tom, who would doubtless pursue Charlie's already well-trampled path – and with less carefully placed steps! Ultimately, indecisiveness decided the question. It became too late to cancel with any degree of decency.

***

Dear Jeremy,

I am too excited not to let you know that your father has agreed to spending next Chinese New Year in London! He has told me to go ahead with booking our flights and making our reservations. Of course, I have not yet discussed with him details of whom we should ask to join us and whom we should visit during our stay but I am hopeful that this trip will help us all to re-establish our loving family relationships.

It is with this in mind that I am writing and hoping that you will be happy to return to a regular exchange of letters, rather like when you were at school. This would mean so much to me and it would help me when the time comes for me to prepare your Dad for catching-up with you.

*It is so long since it has been possible for you to tell us of your progress with your studies. Your PhD must, by now, be two-thirds completed. How exciting it will be when you have finished. **Dr.** Chan: such pride!*

Coming back to New Year and ever-mindful of a need for careful planning, I was wondering if you agree with my feeling that a meal shared with friends would make for an altogether easier occasion. I have in mind your two old chums, Tom and Harry, whose families were so hospitable to you during your school years and, of course, Mr. Charlie is forever in our debt. How lovely it would be to see him, once more!

But I am allowing my enthusiasm to get the better of me, and I realise that February is still so far away, thus I shall not pester *you with more detail, yet. Do, please, let me know what you think and do,do,do tell me (eventually, **us**!) what is happening in your studies.*

All my love (& on your Dad's behalf),

Mom. xxx.

***

Jeremy read Geraldine's letter on the train. He returned it to its envelope, deliberately, slipping it into an inside breast pocket of his jacket, and looking through the window at the passing countryside. Fields full of maturing lambs; trees cloaked in mid-summer foliage, causing lozenges of light to dapple on the grass beneath their awnings; suburban gardens, their flower-beds aglow with colour, their lawns trimmed and striped; 'A' roads and motorways carrying an ever-intricate ballet of cars overtaking lorries as the train, itself, overtook all with which it ran parallel. It was the multifaceted complexity of human existence that preoccupied Jeremy's thoughts and a gathering, acidic nausea that gnawed within his belly.

Tom met him at the station. "Beer-o'-clock, I reckon!" he declared, falsely checking his watch and with that open cheerfulness that had melted Jeremy's oriental reserve, when they had all first met in the Day Room at school, exchanging one another's brief autobiographies with varying degrees of caution and devil-may-care. "I know just the place for a swift starter-for-ten! This way. No dragging of the feet; ale awaits!"

It being a Friday, the pub was heaving, already. Tom knew, instinctively, where to find a space that would accommodate them and he burrowed through the bodies, like a nippy three-quarter jinxing his way through a floundering loose scrum. This had been his party-piece on the rugby pitch. Unlike Harry, he had never been a devotee but he did have natural ability. He re-surfaced, yards away from the point at which he had entered, gathered-up a couple of unoccupied stools, which he almost cuddled, protectively, popped them into a convenient gap, and shouted, "Mine's a cold one; I'll guard the fort!" Jeremy made a less dramatic move towards the bar and secured their drinks.

Tom had planned his campaign, carefully. He intended to betray not one iota of concern for his friend. He knew Jeremy too well: this would be tantamount to flashing a *Danger. Beware!* signal at him. The rope holding-up his portcullis would be severed, instantly, and down it would smash, holding the enemy at bay. If Tom were to successfully inveigle his way into the inner sanctum that was Jeremy's true self, ingenuity must be deployed. He had the whole weekend at his disposal and he was content to use as much of it as was necessary.

"*Ecce homo*! Behold, a man triumphant, bearing the spoils of war! Come, brave and noble warrior, take your ease and sup!" When Tom was in this frame of mind, be it genuine or feigned, his good humour was irresistible. Jeremy had not the slightest inkling that his bastions, even now, were under siege.

An Exchange of Courtesies.

Despite its bizarre conclusion, Charlie Wimpole could not deny that Sir William's dinner party had been sumptuous. His social programming made it impossible for him not to write a letter of thanks, almost immediately upon his return to school. In it, he alluded to his now imminent retirement; to the array of differing social opportunities his post had availed him, over the years; finally, to the unique combination of mediaeval largesse and post-modern gallimaufry Sir William had presented to him. He was satisfied that the letter balanced wit with sincerity; individual politeness with generic propriety.

Sir William was pleased to receive it. Pleased, as would be any host, that his efforts were acknowledged; pleased that it offered him a reason to establish renewed contact. "Letter to Charles Wimpole, Esq., address on file," he spoke into his Dictaphone. *Dear Charles, I do not make a habit of writing to thank folk for their thank you letters but, on this occasion, I must make an exception. It was good of you, indeed, to ignore the discourtesies heaped upon you, towards the end of our gathering. They still weigh heavily upon my conscience.*

I should imagine, also, that your breakfast conversation did nothing to resolve the enigma into which you must feel you have inadvertently wandered. I feel that you are owed some clarification. Would it be convenient for you to join me at my club either this coming Thursday or Friday? I am required in London for a few days but I am free on either of those two evenings.

I appreciate that the combination of packing, routine end of term duties, and, no doubt, a plethora of invitations finds your time much curtailed but your agreement to meet would be much appreciated. "Yours, etc. To be dispatched, first class, today, please."

***

As Jeremy travelled south to meet Tom, Charlie travelled north to meet Sir William. Unbeknownst, they were both targets of their hosts.

Charlie announced his name and that of the member who had invited him to the desk porter. A list was checked. A polite but firm request to sign-in was made and the door-lock was released. "Sir William is awaiting you at the bar, sir." Charlie was reassured, "Straight ahead, sir, followed by right and right again. You will pass a cloakroom on your left, should you require it. Thank you very much, sir." No habitué of Club land, Charlie was amused by the rote-learned niceties of the staff.

Sir William was in conversation with a small group at the bar and, having secured him a drink, he incorporated Charlie into the circle with practised ease. As the level in the glass lowered, he suggested a freshener and, with equal panache, detached the pair of them from the circle and guided Charlie to a comfortable corner, designed for greater privacy. However, he seemed to be in no hurry to open the bidding. Seamlessly, he sashayed from subject to subject, guiding Charlie through a sequence of interesting topics without his ever feeling the slightest pressure or direction. This continued, once they had climbed the extravagant staircase, which led to the restaurant on the first floor, and settled at their table. The Head Waiter met them, as they entered, and surprised Charlie, not so much by being able to address Sir William by name but himself, also. "Good evening, Sir William; good evening Mr. Wimpole, I hope you enjoy your first visit to the club. I have reserved a corner table for you; it's very discreet," he assured them, as he glided through the labyrinth of tables, towards a large bay window and a table set for two, nestling into the right-angle formed with the neighbouring wall.

Sophisticated trivia accompanied their inspection of the menu and their first course. Not until a first mouthful of the main dish had been tasted and judged did Sir William manoeuvre himself into business mode. "You may be aware that young Chan took considerable exception to your not being invited to attend Professor Tinniswood's presentation, the other evening," was his opening gambit. "Evidently, and quite understandably, he holds you in high regard." Charlie decided to restrict his comments to the minimum that courtesy dictated. He understood that he had been invited to listen, rather than to speak. "Are you apprised of his most recent gesture of disapproval, by any chance?"

"If you mean has he told me of his intention to abandon his PhD, the answer is yes, I am."

"And your view of this?" Sir William gently coaxed.

"I told him that I thought he was making a huge mistake. I did my best to dissuade him."

"Ah." Sir William followed this gnomic monosyllable with a draft of wine, which he savoured, swallowing it slowly. He then addressed his attention to the plate of food in front of him, re-loading his fork and relishing the portion he placed in his mouth.

"When you say that you did your best to dissuade him, may I take it that you are not convinced that you were entirely successful?"

"I know I was unsuccessful," replied Charlie with the simple honesty he had determined upon, perhaps as a subconscious foil to Sir William's preferred super-subtlety.

"Did that surprise you? Had you expected to bring your view to bear?"

"If you mean had I assumed that the ex-pupil would do his ex-housemaster's bidding, your grasp of how twenty-first century education operates is uncharacteristically adrift!" He had felt unable to resist this and, even if the phraseology had betrayed a more combative nature than he had intended to reveal, the essential truth remained untainted.

"Touché! 'A hit, a very palpable hit!' So, would you say that your powers of persuasion operate within limited parameters – regarding both current and former pupils?"

"I would say that anyone's powers of persuasion operate within limited parameters - or, at least, that they should do. More is tyranny." He mirrored Sir William's use of the wine glass and loaded fork for emphasis.

"But what if you *know* you are in the right?"

"To *believe* that one is in the right, imposes upon one a duty to try one's hardest to explain why. If one fails, there is no more to be done about it."

"What if I were to describe that as effete liberalism?" Sir William's tone had not changed but a blaze had entered his eyes which Charlie recognised to be the true indicator of his dining companion's feelings, regardless of the well-trained control over his voice.

"One man's effete liberalism is another man's free-will! Call it what you like, it may be inconvenient and infuriating but it's a damn sight better than the alternative!"

"And what would you describe the alternative to be?"

"Totalitarianism!"

"So you would say that it is wrong for the parent who knows (*believes*, if you prefer) that a child is about to eat something that will harm it to remove the source of danger, if the child refuses to listen to a warning given?"

"I would say that you have selected an example that has no bearing upon the issue we met to discuss." It was a spontaneous but, nonetheless, perfectly formed comment.

"Would you care for dessert or cheese, gentlemen?" Their cleared main course plates had been removed, crumbs had been swept from the table-cloth, the bottle had been emptied and removed.

"I always feel the club offers a sufficiently substantial main course to obviate the need for anything further, myself. Or would you care for more?" He had done it again!

"No more for me, thanks. That was superb."

"We'll take coffee in the Library. Thank you." He allowed a few seconds to pass and for the waiter to retreat before standing. "Shall we?" he proffered, and, once again, Charlie saw Sir William's extended arm as a direction post.

Once more, they alighted upon the serpentine staircase, effortlessly sweeping to the floor below. The Library was precisely as Charlie had anticipated: floor-to-ceiling stacks of largely undisturbed volumes, soft, slightly scuffed, leather chairs, fans of newspapers and glossy magazines displayed upon occasional table tops.

Sir William asked Charlie what he would like to accompany his coffee. Both were drunk, appreciatively, accompanied by an inconsequential history of the club. Evidently, Sir William had no intention of returning to the wider topic of Free Will, nor to the more specific one of Jeremy Chan. Charlie had hoped that he might learn more about the true cause of Jeremy's anxiety; indeed, he had anticipated that Sir William planned to take him into his confidence. But he had not been sufficiently servile; nor had he proved to be as compliant as perceived. Sir William had misjudged his intended bag, having stalked it. He considered the prize unworthy of the ammunition's cost.

"I'm staying the night. May I ask the desk-porter to secure you a taxi, or do you prefer to walk?"

"I'm a plodder, by nature, Sir William. Thank you, but I am happy to walk."

"Not nearly plodding enough!" thought Sir William, as he escorted Charlie to the front entrance, shook his hand, and bad him goodnight. He returned to the Library, having ordered another large Irish Malt.   A determination bordering upon ruthlessness suffused his face.

Out On The Town!

"What viands, i'faith?" Tom was still in cod literary mode. "The world's fare may be furnished forth upon Londinium's table! Locusts from Laos; Patagonian Porcupine; South Somalian Surprise - I can guide you where your appetite dictates!" Whilst they were now in their third pub, and although it appeared that he was well on his way towards oblivion, Tom had been almost scientifically pacing himself. He had always been a good actor and, once in character, he was totally credible. "Cuisine: urban, pastoral, aqueous; avian, mammalian, piscatorial; cereals, legumes, roots; fruits, false and true. Come try, come try!" It was a bravura performance.

Jeremy had left Cambridge clear of mind and purpose: he would honour Tom's invitation, as friends should honour each other. He would force his troubles to the darkest recess of his mind and memory. He would be a better guest than he had been a host to Charlie. He would permit nothing to intrude upon a well-intended invitation. But then, settled in his carriage, he had read his mother's letter. First Hermione, then Geraldine. It was as if they were in league against him! Once again that warning voice whispered into his inner-ear. But how difficult it was for someone who was *actually* facing emotional entrapment to avoid the accusation of paranoia!

Tom's ebullience was infectious. The drinks were going down *so* smoothly. He felt happier than he could remember. "Let's push the boat out!" he enthused, "I vote for wonderful over weird! Hit me with *the very best* Italian restaurant you can muster!" Tom disengaged from his Motley Fool caricature, briefly, to make a call. His negotiating skills were extended to their limit but he emerged, triumphant. "Jeremy Chan: prepare to be amazed; prepare to be utterly, flabberghastedly, amazed! No time to tarry; we must sally forth!" He had rediscovered his stride.

Whilst his principal purpose was to discover the PIN to Jeremy's troubling secret, his genuine concern for his friend's well-being demanded that, whatever chicanery he may be guilty of, he should do nothing to undermine the firmly established structure of that friendship. His earlier ploy to get Jeremy wasted was now re-addressed. City Boy, though he had become, he still recognised the real value of money and, most especially, for those who earned far less than he did, himself. They were bound for a *top* establishment. It would cost. It would, also, be wonderful. It was not an experience to be abused. Quietly negotiating with the taxi driver, he bought them a roundabout route. He was now embarked upon a balancing act as delicate as any the circus had to offer: the mood of bonhomie must be maintained but not allowed to tip over into 'lager-and-curry-territory'. Neither could he risk it becoming tarnished with the taint of 'peaked-too-soon'. As they made their way, Tom endeavoured to remove the metaphorical Cap and Bells, whilst retaining the ambience of top form. It required an adroitness that few could have mustered.

He decided that enthusiasm was his surest way. He enthused about the location they were heading towards; he enthused about the food, the wine list, the service, the clientele. He could not have bettered his efforts if he had been employed to promote the restaurant's fortune.

And he pitched it perfectly. The journey had given him opportunity to modify his earlier excess without raising questions; he had engaged Jeremy's attention and prompted Jeremy's laughter, throughout. Both were hungry and in a mind to sample some serious dining pleasure.

***

Thousands of miles eastwards, Gerald and Geraldine were fast asleep. They, too, had enjoyed a wonderful night out. Slowly, slowly, friends had realised that their withdrawal, whatever may have been its cause, had come to an end. Geraldine, whom they recognised to have been the worst affected, seemed to be back to her old self. They negotiated with each other, seeking an occasion that would both reinstate Gerald and Geraldine's position within their social circle but avoid making it seem too obvious. It was a beautifully conceived conundrum and beautifully resolved.

A significant wedding anniversary offered the opportunity. The invitation was delicately phrased: *Gerald & Geraldine: we have been married for only one year less than we have known you both. This makes you our longest-standing friends in KL. How could we contemplate celebrating without you? We do hope you will be able to join us.* The tone was relaxed without being careless; the emotional pitch was warm but not stifling; there was a call for a positive response without it seeming a plea. Both had been delighted to receive it. They, too, had been wondering quite how to return to their social circle without the need to explain. This was perfect.

They had enjoyed such a lovely evening: as much food as they could manage; as much chat as they had exchanged in months.

Upon returning home, they were tired, but not exhausted. They had rediscovered contentment. As they were preparing for bed, Gerald asked Geraldine how she was progressing with her plans for New Year. She told him that the fights were booked and that the hotel reservations had been made. She then felt her heart in her mouth. Was this, she wondered, the time she had so patiently waited for? Should she take her opportunity or was it still too soon after they had both started to feel so much better? She kept their conversation alive, steering it towards the fun they had enjoyed, the value of friendship, the need for a degree of permanency in life. She then began to think: "Gerald's not stupid. I've taken the conversation this far. Not to mention Jeremy would be to highlight the omission. It would be unnatural of me. He would wonder why I had not. How I could not. I must." As she folded-back the top sheet, a light covering for the still-humid summer weather, she tried to replicate its lightness in her voice. "I've been wondering about our entertaining in London," she ventured. "Chinese friends will need to know that we are planning to visit, so as to ensure they are not double-booked. It is always lovely to mix-in our English friends, too. We must let Jeremy know, of course." It was done; it had been said; there was no retreat. She was not even sure whether she had chosen "must" and "of course" or if they had merely emerged as part of the sentence she was speaking. Certainly, if the former and in retrospect, it had been a brave choice. "Ought" would have invited discussion; "must" and "of course" made none necessary.

Gerald was settling. He was looking forward to a good sleep. He was happy to half-listen to his wife's plans, comfortable in the knowledge that they were her particular area of expertise. "Whatever you think best," he murmured, and then drifted into sleep. Geraldine's heart was beating so rapidly that she lay still for a full hour before she, too, succumbed. Could it be that their family crisis was over? Oh, how she hoped it was!

***

"*That*, Tom, was *the* best meal I have *ever* had! Wow, *what* a set-up!"

Tom knew that Jeremy was right. It had been astonishing. They had eaten, and they had drunk, and they had talked, and talked, and talked. Had not the most discreet of waiters delicately indicated that no other diners remained, it would not have occurred to either of them to call for the bill. The cost was phenomenal. But it had been worth it.

They were now back at Tom's flat. Jeremy had not felt this relaxed for longer than he could remember. Tom had to admit to himself that his mission remained merely an intention. He knew that Jeremy had decided to abandon his PhD. But he did not understand why and he had been sufficiently self-disciplined neither to contest the decision nor to seek-out the reason. It was still only the early hours of Sunday morning. Jeremy was not going to leave for Cambridge until Monday morning, when Tom set-off for work. There was time, yet, and, perhaps more importantly, he appeared to have secured Jeremy's confidence - something he regretted Charlie had failed to do: the unhappy terms of his departure, a fortnight ago, had emerged. Depending upon how much further progress he made, he may well decide to exchange notes with Charlie W. "Time to kip?" he asked, casually. "We should make the most of tomorrow."

"Verily, to boot, yay, and forsooth!" concurred Jeremy, capping Tom's earlier, much earlier, cod Olde Englisshe. "How wonderful to spend an evening with someone who has no agenda!" he thought, as he crashed onto the sofa-bed Tom had prepared for him.

It's A Waiting Game.

"Thanks for a *great* weekend, Tom!   Let's plan to get Harry down and re-visit that restaurant - once the bank balance had been resuscitated!"   They took their different tube lines: he to Liverpool Street; Tom to Bank.   Unwittingly, he took with him, also, the unrevealed secret that Tom had been so determined to discover.

***

Geraldine had hoped for a prompt response from her son.   None arrived.   It was a disappointment she had to internalise.   She could not afford to jeopardise the progress she had made by admitting to Gerald that she had written.   She attempted to reassure herself by focussing upon the benefits her patience, thus far, had accrued.   She must not seem to be insistent towards Jeremy; she must trust that a reply *would* come, in time.

***

Hermione, also, awaited a reply to *her* letter.   Whilst she acknowledged that she had offered Jeremy as much time as he needed to recognise the error he was making, she confessed that she had hoped it would take him hardly any time at all!

***

Whilst he felt able to congratulate himself upon the supreme self-discipline he had exercised over the weekend, Tom was disconsolate.   True, he knew a little more than he had before Jeremy's visit but he was all too well aware that he was no nearer

- 206 -

the quick of the issue than he had ever been. Surrender was not a word that featured in his vocabulary. But consultation was. He decided that he would contact Charlie W. They needed to form an alliance in this campaign.

***

Normally the personification of charming urbanity, Sir William's mood, following his return from London, was not sweet. He had been worsted. It was not an experience to which he was much used, nor was it one he relished. "No interruptions this morning, please!" he peremptorily instructed his p.a., disappearing briskly into his office. His diction had been courteous enough but its register had resonated ire.

He removed his cell phone from its jacket-pocket-pouch. For this call, he calculated, the landline (no matter how secure) was inappropriate. Having punched-in the requisite numbers, it was only a split second before he was talking. "William Abercrombie, here. I have a job for you." Evidently, this was no social call. His tone was crisp; his directions crystalline. "I'll await your findings, then. Make them good; make them swift; make them stick. Good morning." He was done.

***

Tom telephoned Charlie as soon as he returned from work.

"Tom! How good to hear from you. How's tricks?"

"I'll cut straight to the chase, Charlie: it's Jeremy I'm phoning about. I'm concerned that things are far from being right with him."

"Ah, yes. I fear that you may well be right."

"Can we swap notes?"

"I'm not sure I've much to tell you that you won't have fathomed for yourself but neither have I signed-up to any privacy clause in my chats with him, so: yes, by all means – especially if the two of us can sort him out."

"I'm free, this Saturday. Could we meet? I know you must be hellishly busy but I think there's something really bad going on."

"Busy? Are you spelling that m a n i c?! But, no, you're right. I'm at Farewell Speeches in the evening but I could manage lunch and the p.m."

"Great! I'll come down to you and save you yet more hassle. Would *The Royal Oak* at about one-ish suit?"

"Spot on! I'll see you there."

As Charlie had suggested, they both knew much the same as each other. Or, more significantly, neither knew what lay at the heart of Jeremy's problem. "One weird thing he asked me, when he visited over the reunion weekend, concerned the punishment that might be meted-out to anyone found to be guilty of forcing another to break The Official Secrets' Act. I know it sounds very melodramatic, but he seemed so serious."

"What did you say?"

"I just told him that I had no idea. Then, when I tried to pursue it further, he clammed-up."

"Do you think he might have been made to sign it? I've no idea what his research involves but, when he first started, he did tell me that he had been appointed to a pretty off-beam supervisor, who operated from an isolated base. I agree, it all sounds too Le Carre to be true, but you never know."

"OK, so let's assume he has signed the Act. That he has stumbled upon something he considers to be wrong. That he feels constrained to distance himself from it but unable to explain himself. Where do *we* go from *there*?"

And so they skated around and around the rink of hypothesis until Charlie glimpsed his watch. "Christ! Is that really the time? I'm sorry, Tom, I'll have to go. To miss one's own retirement presentation may be considered by some to be the height of poor taste! Look, we'll keep in touch. I realise that we've got nowhere, today, but there *must* be a way! Could you give me a swift lift back?"

***

As his train pulled out of Liverpool Street, Jeremy pulled the envelope containing his mother's letter from his breast pocket. He re-read it. Twice. Three times. "**Dr.** Chan: such pride!" Anyone who might say that irony was merely a literary device hadn't the first notion! How could he possibly tell her? Then there was that other letter lying on his desk, unanswered. What more was there to say for Hermione to pass-on to Quentin? As a Scientist, he welcomed questions and he had long-since decided to devote his life to answering them. But *these* questions! They *had* no satisfactory answers! He found himself cast in the role of infidelity *because* he valued honesty. Not only irony, but paradox, too!

"What next?" he wondered. "Search me!" he concluded. Once again, he was looking out of the window. The lambs, the trees, the gardens, the traffic were as they had been on the way down. So, too, was he: utterly confounded.

A Well-Hatched Plot.

The envelope was marked "Personal", thus Sir William's p.a. avoided opening it. She placed it on top of the pile of correspondence which she then took into his office.

"Thank you. No need to wait; I'll buzz you, if necessary." As soon as she had left the room, he snapped-up the envelope, took a paper-knife and slit it open, as if he were filleting a fish. He gave the letter his full concentration. Then he dived into his jacket pocket, removed his cell phone and dialled. "Abercrombie, here. Good work! Remuneration will follow." Whether he was talking to a person or to a voice-mail machine, he was purposeful to the point of being curt. He ignored the remaining pieces of correspondence and turned his attention to his lap-top. Next, he sent an email to Quentin: *Q. – We have our "other route". Call in. W.* Cryptic though it was, Quentin understood. He lifted his telephone. "Oh, good morning, Quentin Tinniswood, here, may I make an appointment with Sir William, please? It's quite urgent. This afternoon? That would be excellent! I'll be with you for two-thirty prompt; many thanks." Having replaced the receiver, he paused, briefly, and inhaled deeply, releasing his breath in one long, controlled, profound action. "Hermione," he called across the lab., "I'm summoned to The Star Chamber! I fear for our young friend but I shall do my best."

True to his word, Quentin arrived at two-thirty, precisely. Accuracy was a concept he found himself comfortable with - unlike the concept of plotting, which he surmised he would be grappling with soon. He did not have long to wait before he was escorted into Sir William's office.

"The Housemaster proved to be a waste of time and effort," Sir William launched-in pretty well where they had left-off, last time. "*But* a far more exotic prospect beckons! One Anita del Azura: an MPhil in Politics; a citizen of Cuba; an erstwhile lover of Jeremy Chan, loose cannon!" The Deputy Vice-Chancellor allowed himself a moment's smugness.

"She's returned home. And, as you say, they have split-up."

"What a dear, genuine, romantic innocent you are, Quentin! It's a good job you've had Hermione to keep you on the broad and crooked, all these years!"

"I don't understand."

"Demonstrably! Listen and learn, my friend! We have a problem: a young man so disapproves of a project which we cherish that he is prepared to commit academic and professional suicide, in order to detach himself from it. Let us change his metaphor: loose cannon, no longer, but stray sheep. The unknown potential embrace of our problem would be conveniently restricted were we to find a means of restoring the stray sheep to its fold. Now, why might the Cuban Government have expended some of its all-too-spartan funding upon the higher education of a denizen of one of its principal families? I think we can dismiss both nepotism and corruption. Neither sits easily with ideology! Whilst Capitalism may be anathema in Cuba, the concept of investment is not - thus their world-renowned Health Service. Money was not *expended* upon Anita del Azura's education; it was *invested*. Invested in *her*, personally. Were the resultant contribution to her society to be rendered nugatory, that would be ..." here, he paused, in order to select the precise word he wanted and then he continued, carefully articulating it: "unfortunate. 'Reputation, reputation, reputation! O, I have lost my reputation! I have lost the immortal part of myself, and what remains is bestial!' Shakespeare knew the potency of reputation, Quentin. Politicians within any system of government depend upon their reputation. To lose this is to lose all. The custodian of Anita del Azura's reputation is Jeremy Chan – or, at least, such would be credible. Do you recall the reference I requested from that bloody Housemaster chappie? It is the *one* useful function he has served. Brief though it was, it contained a vital comment. Wimpole invoked Biblical authority and proclaimed young Chan to be 'Honest and of good report.' Not a cad who would countenance the loss of his former lover's reputation. He may not know it - yet - but he is, indeed, that reputation's custodian. He will wish, I am sure, to exercise his responsibility dutifully." It had been something of a *tour de force*. Sir William appeared to be satisfied with the manner in which he had presented his thoughts. He placed his hands in his lap and rested his gaze upon Quentin.

Quentin had, indeed, listened. And he had learned. Learned that Machiavellianism was extant, not extinct.

"How do you propose that Jeremy should be made aware of his new role?"

"Oh, I think that would be best coming from you. Or from Hermione, if you prefer."

"But he no longer attends the lab."

"A paltry evasion, Quentin; shame on you!"

"Hermione's already written to him. There's been no response."

"I think you'll find he'll respond to this information. Charlie Wimpole may be less-than-cooperative but he knows his former pupils well. What he tells us of Chan's nature will prove to be true. Indeed, it already has: why else do you think he's willing to jettison a future that was once assured?"

Quentin had promised Hermione that he would do his best. In these circumstances, his best had proved to be simply not good enough. He could perceive no alternative to compliance.

"Not to be too insistent, Quentin, but I really *do* think you would be wise to act immediately. This evening would be ideal. And now I think we can safely say there's no more to consider, at present." The master of dismissal had demonstrated his craft, once more.

A Home Visit.

Quentin and Hermione decided that it would be best for them to convey Sir William's dark message together. They also decided that a letter would be an inadequate medium. Whilst they genuinely believed Jeremy to be wrong, they wished him no ill.

Hermione took the view that they should chance an unannounced visit to his flat. Not that she wanted to catch him unawares but because she feared a request to visit might be turned down.

They left the lab. earlier than usual and made their way towards where they knew Jeremy to live, although they had not been there, before. Their intention was to arrive before he may have started preparing himself an evening meal. If they could persuade him, they would like to take him out to dinner. But they realised that he may consider this to be inappropriate. They harboured a deep fear that their desire to help may be misconstrued.

Inevitably, Jeremy was surprised at anyone ringing his buzzer, let alone them. However, he pressed the door release button and welcomed them in. If nothing else, he thought, this would resolve the problem of what to do about Hermione's letter. They were both nervous and embarrassed. They knew that their mission could not be presented in any light other than one of brutal clarity. They established that they were not playing the part of apologists for Sir William and that they would understand if Jeremy held their preparedness to act as his messengers in contempt. And then they told him what they were charged to say.

Having both witnessed his eruption at Quentin's presentation, they were fearful that there may be a repetition. But no such reaction occurred. Indeed, recognising their anxiety, Jeremy reassured them that it would not. It had been triggered by the way in which Charlie had been treated, he explained, not by what Quentin had to say. His response to them was calm. Not coldly calm. Not calm in the unsettling way that men like Sir William were able to conjure-up. He was mildly calm. Even generously so. "What an unmitigated, utter, total and complete bastard!" was never uttered with so little malice.

"Listen, you must stay for supper," he unexpectedly proposed. Rather than having wrong-footed him, as they had feared, they seemed to have re-directed him. Jeremy-becalmed had become Jeremy-with-sails-full-furled.

He found some gin and fixed them each a drink. He dived into his freezer and emerged, bearing several solid containers, the first of which he fed into the micro-wave. "I'll start some gentle de-frosting but I take it there's no rush." It was as if the difficulties of the past few weeks had never existed. His manner towards them was as it had been when first he started to work under Quentin's supervision. It was uncanny, yet it appeared to be no act.

With some degree of trepidation, the central issue having been somewhat sidelined, Quentin observed, "Of course, sadly, I am obliged to report back. What should I tell him?" He prepared himself to hear, "You can tell him from me to fuck-off!" But it didn't happen.

"Tell him that I would like to meet with him in his office, if you would." There was a serenity about his words that belied their context. It was as if he were the driver, not the driven. "Tell him that I wish no man ill – nor any woman, either! Tell him that I am not the stroppy student he imagines; that I understand where my bread is buttered; when I have been worsted; how to conduct myself appropriately. Yes," he paused, "tell him that, emphatically." It was a judicious coda. Quentin could hardly believe his ears. Hermione's blue eyes misted-over. It was like a scene from a movie. The speech, spontaneous though it was, glistened with the polish of multiple re-writes. "Now, let me refresh your glasses."

Supper followed. Then coffee. They did not leave until nearly midnight. They were able, honestly, to say, "Thank you, Jeremy. Thank you, *so much*. It's been a *wonderful* evening." There was a sore temptation to add, "When will we see you, next?" But both were wiser than that.

Resolute.

Dear Tom & Charlie,

Forgive this plurality but I am anxious to establish what the politicians call 'transparency' – who could be more transparent than they, flimsy and superficial creatures?!

You are both owed explanations (you, especially, Charlie, following my appalling behaviour, the other week.) I suspect that I should, perhaps, have made this a tri-partite letter and included Harry but, as ever, his interest in my well-being has been rather more understated than yours. Please feel free to share with him, as you think appropriate.

You will be pleased to know that my malaise, which arose out of uncertainty, is passed. I am uncertain, no more. (I feel like a nineteenth century heroine, declaring herself no longer a virgin! But there it is.)

I have been foolish. Academic ambition allowed me to lose my way for a while. I signed a document that I ought to have had sense enough to eschew. It is a form of contract that should not be broken. Part of my uncertainty revolved around whether or not I should pay regard to that fact. This is at the centre of my new-found resolve.

I began by promising clarification; already, I am guilty of continued obfuscation! Mea culpa. Mea maxima culpa!

As a pre-requisite of my PhD research I was obliged to sign The Official Secrets' Act. I now find myself out of sympathy with the direction in which my work has been pointed and, thus, I have indicated my intention to withdraw from it. The man upon whose insistence it was that I signed the Act seeks to prevent me from abandoning my studies and, no doubt, fears that it is my intention to scupper the project. I am due to meet with him in a few days' time. Charlie: you know the man; it is Sir William Abercrombie. At present, I feel confident that this meeting will be one at which misunderstandings may be resolved. This is my preferred outcome. Should it prove otherwise, I know what I must (and will) do.

I shall keep you informed and I thank you for your vigilance.

How's the packing going, Charlie? Do you need some voluntary muscle? If so, you may be assured that I, Harry, and Tom will be happy to flex a few biceps in a good cause (won't we, Tom?)!

All my very best to you both.

As ever,

Jezza.

***

Dear Mom,

I am sorry that this has taken so long. Why it has will become clearer as I go on.

WELL DONE! To coax the Old Man into agreeing to C.N.Y. in London is a triumph! I thought he may <u>never</u> return to UK, following the mayhem of his last visit! I'm sorry that it ended as it did but I'm up for putting all to rights.

BUT (there's always a but!) there is an unavoidable hazard to negotiate.

I have decided not to pursue my PhD any further. I know this will come as a shock and as a huge disappointment but it is unavoidable and it's not up for discussion! This is <u>my</u> decision and not in consequence of my supervisor being discontented with my work. Had it been the latter, you would be right to feel let down; that it is not should be, I would hope, cause to accept that I know what I am doing and that I have my (good) reasons.

There is an up-side to this: I plan to return to KL. It will be before February but you must not let that alter your plans. IF Dad will grant me leave, I will be happy to accompany you. Leave from what? I hear you ask. And rightly. I've put cart before horse! I am very much hoping that I will be able to land a job at the factory. Despite the (unacceptable to me) direction in which my research has been forced, there are others in which it may be taken and they are akin to the factory's operation. Exciting new processes would (note I do not say could!) follow.

Of course, I understand that I am placing a huge burden of responsibility on your shoulders, here. Or do you think it would be wiser/better for me to write, directly, to Dad? I'll be guided by you.

I have loose-ends to tidy-up, here. Once I know when, I'll let you know the date of my return.

Love, as always,

Jeremy.

***

Memo to: Sir William Abercrombie.

From: Jeremy Chan.

Ref.: Our imminent meeting.

Sir William,

- *Professor Tinniswood has kindly conveyed to me the date you have offered for a meeting between us. Happily, I am available.*

- *Despite uncalled-for provocation, my intention is that we should reach an amicable mutuality.*

- *Senorita Anita del Azura and I are no longer emotionally attached but we have managed to secure an enduring friendship. This is an arrangement I will not compromise.*

- *Until recently, the whole of my educational experience in this country has been both nurturing and encouraging. As it draws to an end, may I make clear my hope and expectation that it will not fall short of these admirable intentions.*

- *I look forward to a positive and productive meeting.*

***

Dear Quentin (& Hermione, of course!),

Thank you for letting me know when Sir William could find time to meet me. I have accepted.

I am hopeful that he will recognise that my aim is not to undermine any pet project he may be jealously guarding but, merely, to detach myself from a line of research I find latently repugnant.

In saying this, I do not intend any sleight upon either of you. **You** *are convinced that SPA is morally defensible, a potential life-saver, a break-through in Intelligence that will, one day, be heralded as its acceptable face. I hope, sincerely, that your faith is upheld. It is, however, a faith I cannot share. Has not History taught us that there is little worse that Mankind can impose upon itself than enforced faith? Hermione: your last letter was that of a proselyte; I do not believe, however, that it was intended to be a secular variant upon the Papal Bull! It is my belief that you both understand, even sympathise with, the position I have adopted, even if you do not agree with it. For that, I thank you.*

If all goes well with Sir William, I shall be making arrangements to return home, shortly. Should he be determined to create difficulties, I will be forced to respond accordingly.

I promise to let you know the outcome.

How lovely it was to spend an evening together, recently.

Yours ever,

Jeremy.

***

"You have a stark style, Mr. Chan." Sir William was looking at a piece of paper that Jeremy presumed to be a copy of his pre-meeting memo.

"Bullet-points suit memos, Sir William, in much the same way that sonnets suit love poetry and rhyming couplets suit satire."

"Too much of that bugger, Wimpole, here!" thought Sir William. "That's as maybe but may I take it that you are aware of my Office?"

"I am aware that you are the Deputy Vice-Chancellor of the University, yes sir. I am also aware that you are the author of a cheapskate attempt to morally blackmail me!"

"So much for your expressed desire to wish no man ill - nor woman either!" Sir William had seen-off Cabinet Ministers in his time, he was not about to bow the knee to a twenty-three year old student!

"That you can quote me I consider a compliment, Sir William. Quentin Tinniswood is terrified of you. Hermione, less so. I, you must understand, am most certainly not!" He had deliberately echoed the modulated tones of Sir William, regardless of the words he spoke, or of their import. The Career Diplomat was inwardly infuriated by Jeremy's composure. He was forced to recognise in him his own younger self.

"I've called you here to talk about SPA." He judged a change of direction to be apposite.

"You've *agreed to meet me* here, in response to my request, conveyed to you by Professor Tinniswood, and, itself, prompted by your attempt to use a former relationship of mine as some form of cosh!"

Their eyes met. The engagement lasted for several seconds. Jeremy was determined that he would be neither the first to avert his gaze nor the first to speak next. His will prevailed.

"The purpose and circumstances of our meeting may be open to interpretation, Mr. Chan. May I address SPA, first?"

"By all means, now that you have acknowledged it to be not the only item on our agenda."

"Very well. I believe SPA to be, potentially, *the* most significant scientific contribution to Global Intelligence since .... well, quite possibly, since ever. Once its implications are acknowledged – and they *will be* – it is not fanciful to forecast a Nobel Peace Prize for Quentin Tinniswood. He is not a man likely to fail to recognise those who have played their part."

"I wish him well."

"And you do not wish to be part of his success?"

"I do not wish to be part of a process I find to be morally flawed."

"How precious of you! *Life*, Mr. Chan, is morally flawed. Do you not wish to be part of *that* process?"

"Life, at least in its human form, is predicated upon the concept of choice. I *choose* not to be part of that process called SPA."

"You lost the right to choose the day you signed The Official Secrets' Act!" Were he a fencer, this would be a thrust.

Jeremy parried. "Are you telling me that this Act removes any access to the choices I once enjoyed? Are you telling me that such a state of affairs is something the British Government would be happy to acknowledge? Are you telling me that *you*, Sir William Abercrombie, (a signatory if ever I met one!) have lost the right to choose?"

His barrage of questions was met with silence.

On this occasion, Jeremy deemed it best that he should speak next. "I'll tell you what *I* think the Act demands. It demands that I should not reveal anything to any non-designated authority about what I know, regarding SPA. End of! My signature confirms my promise (vow, oath, if you like) to comply with that binding obligation. It does *not* say that I have lost the right to choose bitter over lager, blue over red, insignificance over laureate association."

"But can you be trusted, Mr. Chan?"

"Can I be trusted not to break the speed limit? Can I be trusted not to rob a bank? Can I be trusted not to rape, or to murder? *You* don't know. It's not *your* responsibility. But does the fact that you don't and it isn't mean that I can't drive a car, can't go into town, can't mix with the public at large? There are *laws* which, if transgressed, will bring me to justice. I have agreed to abide by a law. The assumption must be that I *shall* abide by it. Only if I were to break it should I expect to find myself to be in jeopardy. If my signature was not enough for you, Sir William, I tell you now: *I have no intention whatsoever of revealing what I know about SPA. I never have. I simply no longer wish to be part of the project!* Now, *you* tell *me* something: is that too much for you to believe; to acknowledge; to accept?"

"I apologise for my thoughts regarding Miss Azura. May I assure you that they will not be pursued?"

"You've ignored my question, Sir William. I will not answer yours until you've answered mine."

The Deputy Vice-Chancellor rose from his chair. He sauntered towards the bay window and looked–out over the streetscape which lay beyond. He had run out of chips and he knew it. He had to play the percentage game, loathe though he was to submit. To share the spoils was his only reasonable option. He turned back into the room. "Very well, Mr. Chan. Yes, I *can* accept that you are not minded to betray the sensitive and vital knowledge you possess. Will you accept that Miss Azura's political reputation in Cuba will never be tarnished at *my* bidding?"

Jeremy was not going to give him the satisfaction of grasping his opportunity. Although he knew nothing of the meal Charlie W. had shared with Sir William, at his club, he pursued the identical tactic selected by Charlie on that occasion. He mirrored Sir William. To rise and to stroll would have been too obvious. He merely sat and considered. After a few minutes, he looked up and declared without hesitation: "Yes, I'll accept that undertaking." Then he rose, advanced towards Sir William, proffered his hand, shook, and made towards the door. Before he reached it, he turned and said, with a boyish grin, "For a moment, there, I wondered if you were minded to make me the subject of SPA's first clinical trial!"

Sir William demurred from admitting that it had crossed his mind.

Charlie Wimpole had accepted Jeremy's volunteering of his, Tom's and Harry's muscle power. Fifty boxes of books are not easy for one middle-aged man to move. In order to avoid embarrassment, Tom had called Harry and explained what he and Charlie had managed to fathom, regarding Jeremy's anxieties. Jeremy, himself, had ensured that the other three were apprised of his exchange with Sir William. He had also told Quentin and Hermione. She had found it difficult not to betray her delight in the prospect of the Deputy Vice-Chancellor's discomfiture.

"Well, Charlie, you're good to go!" The rooms were bare. No paintings. No books. No ornaments. Almost all the furniture removed. It was a career, almost a life, stripped bare. "Pub-time, I reckon." Jeremy, sensitive as ever, looked at the emptiness and knew that it was no place for Charlie to linger.

"When do wagons roll, tomorrow?" Tom asked.

"Eight-thirty."

"Too early for you to have crashed at mine and then to get back in time to see them off. Let's all put-up at that place we stayed for the reunion weekend. There are bound to be rooms available and it's very reasonable. *This* is fit for no man!" Resonating echoes proved his point. "Are you up for it, Charlie? *Our* treat!"

Charlie looked around the space he had occupied for a significant number of years. Suddenly, it had lost its character, its purpose, its soul. "You're on!" he readily accepted. The prospect of spending even just one night in this emptiness made him shiver. His function, here, had finished; it was time to move on.

***

Dear Jeremy,

I saw your handwriting on the envelope and felt such joy!

I thought you had grown out of being able to surprise me. How wrong I was! However, I have re-read your letter over and over. I trust you to have done what is right.

But what do I tell your father? You know what store he places in education. He always has done. That's why he endured Fothergill's.

I have given it very careful thought. You know that I would never willingly shrink from my responsibilities but, in all honesty, it would be better for <u>you</u> to explain the position to him.

Not to be too negative, I <u>do</u> honestly feel that he will jump at the prospect of your working with him at the factory. For you to ask him if he would be prepared to take you on is, without doubt, the best approach.

I will not ask you for further details about your decision. Perhaps, once you are home, it will all become clearer. I cannot tell you how much I am looking forwards to your return.

All my love,

Mom. xxx

***

"You were a mere boy when last you lived there. So much will have changed. *You* have changed. Will you be happy?" Jeremy had come to say farewell to Quentin and Hermione. His ticket to Malaysia was booked. He had put his flat up for sale. His letter, formally withdrawing from the PhD programme, had been sent to the Head of the Chemical Engineering Department. He had received a strange response, indicating that, perhaps, Professor Tinniswood might not have been the best supervisor to have proposed. He had bothered to reply: *Thank you for your concern but may I be emphatic: Quentin Tinniswood has been an inspirational supervisor. Who knows, one day, the world may well recognise him for the great man he is. I hope it does.* When we do something that is not merely worthy but something which we *know* to be right, we feel something better than satisfaction. We feel warmth. Warmth was what Jeremy felt, as he wrote these words.

"Oh, I think that change and its effects are overemphasised, Hermione. We adapt. I shall be happy, doubt not."

"But is it clear, yet, what you will do?"

"Not exactly. That's my next task. Will you look to take-on another assistant, Quentin?" He needed to deflect attention from himself.

"I've only ever had two assistants and I've taken-on neither! I doubt the Department is likely to guide anyone else in my direction." He paused. He had experienced a momentary flash-back. "Not, that is, unless a Deputy Vice-Chancellor sees fit to intervene." As so often with Quentin, it was difficult to define his tone. Was it whimsical? Bitter? Resigned? Amused, even? Maybe Hermione knew, but even that was unclear.

He had written to Anita. His undertaking to Sir William meant that he had to censor himself but, this notwithstanding, he had managed to convey to her that he had encountered a clash between career and conscience. He hoped that she would approve of his choice. There had been a touching response, in which she applauded the stand he had taken but deplored his decision to become ... *an Industrial Chemist and, by definition, a lackey of the Market Economy!* He had sent a short, slightly waspish, but good humoured riposte: *Do Junior Ministers of State in Cuba work, salary-free? Congratulations upon your recruitment into ethical impurity!* He felt, certainly hoped, that she would detect the redolence of their debating days.

***

Dear Dad,

It must seem - it is a long time since you set-out on your journey to Fothergill's. How I loved those stories, when I was a kid! Best of all was 'The Mistaken Mackintosh'!

You had such courage and a clear purpose in mind: to acquire knowledge that would be useful to your father's business. Against all the odds, you achieved just that. How proud of yourself you must have felt when you returned and applied your knowledge in such a way as to make your father recognise the benefits of the journey you had undertaken. I wonder whether he ever knew of the difficulties you had endured? I doubt you would ever have told him - not even humorously, as you told me.

There was to be no Fothergill's for me. And I thank you for that. 'Mr. Charlie' looked after me well. Cambridge is one of the world's top academic institutions and my life would have been the lesser had I not studied here. Without doubt, the decisions you took on my behalf have changed my life, changed me, in ways that I'm eternally intrigued by, eternally grateful for. But it is time to come home. Time to re-pay, to help you, - if you will allow me to. Time to define, to be me.

The title, 'Dr.' would not have added one jot of benefit to your (may I say our?) factory; the knowledge and the skills I have acquired will. May I have the opportunity to show you, as once you showed your father, how this may be?

I'm so sorry that we parted, last, on such bad terms. It must be hard for you to reconcile what has taken place with what you were brought-up to consider appropriate - acceptable, even. We will need to work at this but I hope that my arrival in KL, next Thursday, will offer us a start. Without a doubt, there is damage to be repaired but I believe that the will to carry-out those repairs lies deep within us both.

Until next Thursday then, Dad.

Your loving son,

Jeremy.

***

No, Chan, Hong-Chun, aka Jeremy, was not Eur-Asian. He had come to recognise that names and places were of little significance. They said nothing that was important. He was the loved and loving son of Gerald and Geraldine. He was the life-long friend of Tom and Harry. He was the beneficiary of Charlie W's kindly care and concern. He was the bright intellectual star and almost surrogate son of Quentin's and Hermione's waning years. He was as good a match on the debating floor as Anita del Azura would ever be likely to encounter in her burgeoning political career – and he had been her lover. A status that he would never regret. He may have enjoyed becoming the scourge of Sir William Abercrombie but he was content to have been, once and briefly, his control. He was ... .

He was himself: the sum total of all that had ever happened to him, thus far in his young life. He aspired, for the time being, to be nothing more and nothing different.

The End.

Printed in Great Britain
by Amazon